KEEPING HER

By Cora Carmack

Keeping Her
Faking It
Losing It

Coming Soon

Finding It

KEEPING HER

A *Losing It* Novella

CORA CARMACK

wm
WILLIAM MORROW
An Imprint of HarperCollins*Publishers*

Excerpt from *Finding It* copyright © 2013 by Cora Carmack.
Excerpt from *Losing It* copyright © 2012, 2013 by Cora Carmack.
Excerpt from *Faking It* copyright © 2013 by Cora Carmack.

EPub Edition SEPTEMBER 2013 ISBN: 9780062299260
Print Edition ISBN: 9780062299277
10 9 8 7 6 5 4 3 2

For Ana
You are going to do so many great things.
And I can't wait to witness them.

And to the #TeamGarrick street team
I pretty much adore you all. And I hope the universe gifts
you each with a gorgeous guy with a lovely accent.

KEEPING HER

1

Garrick

THE ALARM SOUNDED too early.

I smacked it into silence, and then reached for Bliss. I found only rumpled sheets and empty space. My eyelids felt like they'd been weighted down by sandbags, but I sat up and pried them open.

My voice was graveled with sleep when I called out, "Love? Where are you?" Something clanged in the kitchen in response. I sat up, fatigue wiped away by the realization that Bliss was up. And she was cooking.

That couldn't be a good sign.

I threw back the covers, and cool morning air assaulted my bare skin. I pulled on a pair of pajama bottoms and a T-shirt before padding down the hallway to the kitchen.

"Bliss?"

Another clang.

A muttered curse word.

Then I rounded the corner into a war zone.

Her wide eyes met mine. Her face, her hair, our tiny nook of a kitchen was covered in flour. Some kind of batter was smudged across her cheek and the countertops.

"Love?"

"I'm making pancakes." She said it the way one might say, "I didn't do it" when held at gunpoint by policemen. I cast my eyes down to keep from laughing, only to be devastated by the bare legs stretching out from the oversize T-shirt she wore. My T-shirt. Damn.

I'd loved her legs from the moment I'd first seen them while helping her with a burn she'd received on my motorcycle. They drove me to distraction just as much now as they did then.

I could have studied for hours the shape of her thighs and the way they flared out toward her hips. I could have been swept away by the feeling of possession that swelled in me at seeing her wear my clothing. There were dozens of things that I wanted to do in that moment, but an acrid smell tickled my nostrils, and a few tendrils of smoke began to creep around Bliss from the stove at her back. I lurched for the pan, where I found a blackening, misshapen lump of *something*. I pulled the pan off the stove, and heard a slight hitch in Bliss's breath behind me.

Another bad sign.

As quickly as I could, I tossed the "pancake" into the

trash, and deposited the pan in the sink. I said, "Why don't we go out for breakfast?"

Bliss smiled, but it was one of those watery, wavering kinds of smiles that made every man want to run for the hills. I'd become well accustomed to Bliss's panic freak-outs. But crying . . . that was still a terrifyingly unfamiliar territory.

She collapsed into a nearby chair, and her head thumped down onto the table. I stood there, clenching and unclenching my fists, trying to decide on the best course of action. She turned her head to the side, pressing her cheek against the table, and looked at me. Her hair stuck up in every direction, her bottom lip suffered under her teeth, and the look in her eyes pulled at something in my chest. Like an itch at my heart. All I knew was that something was wrong, and I wanted to fix it. The *how* was the question.

I moved forward and knelt beside her chair. Red lined her eyes, and her skin was a shade paler than normal. I asked, "How long have you been awake?"

She shrugged. "Since around four. Maybe closer to three."

I sighed and ran a hand over her unruly hair.

"Bliss . . ."

"I read and did some laundry and cleaned the kitchen." She looked around. "It was clean. I swear."

I laughed and leaned up to press a kiss to her forehead. I pulled another chair around, and took a seat beside her. I laid my head down beside hers, but she closed her eyes and flipped her head around to face the other direction.

She said, "Don't look at me. I'm a mess."

I wasn't about to let her get away with that. I slipped an arm underneath her knees and tugged her into my lap. She whined my name, and then buried her head into my neck. I took hold of her jaw, and made her meet my gaze. It couldn't be a coincidence that this was happening on the day we were set to leave for London to meet my parents. She'd been remarkably calm about it until now. "Everything is going to be fine, love. I swear it."

"What if she hates me?"

That's what this was about. My mother. Bliss could barely handle her own overbearing mother; it seemed cruel that the universe had seen fit to give us two. But I was far more worried about what Bliss would think than what my mother would think. Bliss was honest and sweet and genuine, and my family . . . well, not so much.

I forced a smile and said, "Impossible."

"Garrick, I've overheard enough phone calls with your mother to know she's very . . . opinionated. I'd be stupid not to worry about what she'll think of me."

"You'd be stupid to think that anything my mother could say would matter." And it wouldn't matter to *me*. But it would matter to Bliss. Late at night when our apartment got quiet, the image of my mum as predator and Bliss as prey kept popping into my head. One week. We just had to survive one week. I stroked my thumb across her jaw and added, "I love you."

So much that it terrified me. And I didn't scare easy.

"I know . . . I just—"

"Want her to like you. I know. And she will." *Please God, let my mother like her.* "She'll like you because I love you. She might be a bit abrasive, but like any mother she wants me to be happy."

Or at least I hoped that was how she would see things.

Bliss's chin tipped up slightly, bringing her lips closer to mine. I felt her breath across my mouth, and my body reacted almost instantly. My spine straightened, and I became acutely aware of the bare legs draped across my lap. She said, "And you are? *Happy?*"

God, sometimes I just wanted to shake her. In many ways, she'd overcome the worst of her insecurities, but in moments of stress they seemed to all come rushing back. Rather than wasting my breath answering, I stood with her cradled in my arms, and headed for the hallway.

"What are you doing?" she asked.

I stopped for a moment to press a hard kiss to her mouth. Her fingers laced around my neck, but I pulled back before she could distract me from making my point. "I'm *showing* you how happy I am."

I nudged the bathroom door open, and leaned past the shower curtain. Bliss squealed and held tighter to my neck, as I turned the shower knobs with her still in my arms. She raised an eyebrow, a sly grin sneaking across her lips. "Our shower makes you happy?"

"You make me happy. The shower is just multitasking."

"How very *responsible* of you."

I kissed a smudge of pancake batter off her cheek, and smiled.

"Yes, that's the word."

I set her down on her feet, but her arms stayed tucked around my neck. When she smiled at me like that, I forgot all about the flour on her face or her wild bed head. That smile went straight through me and settled somewhere in my bones.

I kissed her on the forehead and said, "Let's get you cleaned up."

I found the hem of her oversize T-shirt, and began pulling it over her head. I'm not sure where the T-shirt ended up because when I realized she was wearing nothing underneath it, my vision narrowed to encompass only her.

God, she was gorgeous.

If you would have told me two years ago that I'd be getting married to a girl that I'd met just over a year ago, I would have called you mental. My romantic history was so horrendous, I'd never really thought of myself as the marrying type. Until her.

Bliss cleared her throat, and my eyes went back to her. To her mouth. Her chest. The small of her waist that seemed perfectly sculpted to fit in my hands.

She was the ultimate game changer. I hadn't known what it was like to meet a person so full of joy that just by being near her, I was elevated to a happier place. I'd never been with someone who was able to captivate every part of me—mind, body, and soul.

Body, of course, being my primary focus at the moment.

Her bottom lip stuck out, calling to me, and she said, "How long are you going to make me stand here naked while you're fully clothed?"

I took a seat on the toilet, and smiled cheekily up at her. I leaned back, laying one leg across my other knee, and said, "I could do this all day."

And I wasn't lying. I wanted to study her, to memorize her, to be able to close my eyes and see her perfectly as she was.

She rolled her eyes. "Yes, well, it might be a *little* awkward if I were to stay naked *all* day. Though it would make going through airport security much simpler."

I barked a laugh, and she added, "Wasn't your goal to distract me and make me *less* self-conscious? You're falling down on the job, Mr. Taylor."

Well, I couldn't have that, now could I?

I gripped her waist and pulled her forward until my chin brushed the skin just below her belly button. She shivered in my arms, and the reaction sent my blood screaming through my veins. I let my lips graze her just slightly and said, "You have nothing to be self-conscious about."

Her hands laced into my hair, and she looked down at me with glazed eyes. Firmer this time, I dragged my lips over her belly button and up to the valley made by her ribs. I tasted flour on her skin even here, and smothered a laugh.

Above me, she sighed and said, "You're back on track with that distracting thing."

Suddenly impatient, I stood and pulled my shirt over my head. I was rewarded with a breathy sigh and a bitten lip that made it incredibly hard not to be cocky. And not to take her right then.

She swallowed, drawing my eyes to her neck. God, I didn't know what it was about her neck, but it was constantly my undoing. I felt like a teenage boy, wanting to mark that pale, unblemished skin as mine again and again. I brushed a thumb over her pulse point, and she swallowed again, her eyes wide. I laced my fingers through her sleep-addled curls, and tilted her head back.

"How about now?" I asked.

If she was even half as distracted as I was, I'd say I'd done my job. Her eyes pulled away from my bare chest and she said, "Uh . . . what?"

I laughed, but the sound stuck in my throat when her slim fingers smoothed from my chest down to the waist of my pajama bottoms. Her fingers curled around the band, and I swallowed. Looking down, I could see the way her curves reached out toward my body, and I wanted nothing more that to seal our bodies together.

Before I completely lost my train of thought, I said, "No more worrying about my mother, right?"

For either of us.

She gave me a half-glazed glare.

I used one hand to pull her closer, and the other to cup her breast. Then I repeated, "No more worrying."

"Do you promise to do this every time I *do* worry?"

I gave a quick pinch to the tip of the breast in my hand.

She flinched, and then moaned. Her eyes fluttered closed and her body swayed toward mine.

She breathed, "No worrying."

And I thought, *Thank God.*

Because I couldn't wait another second.

I crushed my lips against hers, wishing for the hundredth time that I could just permanently affix our mouths together. Every part of her tasted divine, but her mouth was my favorite. It was so easy to lose myself in kissing her, mostly because I could tell she was doing the same. Her body pressed against mine, and her fingernails dug into my shoulders like she was dangling off a cliff, and that was the only thing holding her up. The harder I kissed her, the harder her nails bit into my skin. I trailed a hand from her neck down the line of her spine, and her mouth broke away from mine. She shivered in my arms, her eyes closed.

I leaned my forehead against hers, and pulled her bare chest to mine. Between the shower steam and her skin, our tiny bathroom felt like a furnace. I never would have thought I could feel such peace while my heart hammered and my skin burned, but that's what she brought me. I'd always thought love was this complicated, messy, frankly ugly thing. Possibly because, growing up, I'd not had much of an example for what a relationship should be. I didn't know it could be any other way. But Bliss chased away the gray and made everything seem black and white. No matter the question, she was the answer.

She was my everything—the lungs that allowed me to

breathe, the heart that had to beat, the eyes that let me see. She'd become a part of me, and all that was left was a piece of paper to tell the world we were as inseparable as I already felt we were.

It was just a piece of paper. The feeling mattered so much more, but a part of me sang with nervous energy demanding we make it official. Soon. It was the same part of me that worried about how Bliss would react to my family . . . to the way I grew up.

She stepped out of my arms, biting down on her already red and swollen bottom lip. Then she pulled back the shower curtain and stepped into the tub.

I hated the fear that chased the heels of my love for her.

Despite the fact that our relationship had begun in the most troubling and impossible situation—between teacher and student—things had been almost perfect since then. A rose-tinted world.

But it couldn't stay that way. Logic, reality, and a lifetime knowledge of my mother made me certain of that. The feeling always came out of nowhere. I'd be watching her, touching her, kissing her, and then suddenly, for one infinitesimal moment I'd feel like it was all about to come crashing down. Like we were balanced on a precipice, it felt inevitable that eventually we would fall. I didn't know how it would happen. Her insecurities. My stubbornness. The interfering hand of fate (or family). But for a few seconds, I could feel it coming.

Then always, she would pull me back. Those seconds of inevitability and uncertainty would dissolve in the sheer magnitude of my feelings for her. The doubt would be erased by the touch of a hand or the quirk of a smile, and I would feel like we could hold off that fall for forever and a day.

She did it again, peeking one last time around the shower curtain wearing nothing but a smile. I heard the water pattern change and knew she'd stepped under the stream of the shower. So I pushed my worries away in favor of a much more pleasant use of my time.

I kicked off the last of my clothing and joined her in the steam. We weren't in London yet, and I wasn't going to let fear steal another second of perfection from my grasp.

As long as we both kept pulling each other back, we'd make it. We'd keep our rose-tinted world.

2

Bliss

OUR MORNING IN the shower turned into a morning back in bed, and that miraculous man loved every ounce of stress from my body. Seriously. I think his tongue had some kind of special ability to melt my bones because I felt so relaxed that I was practically liquid. Just call me Alex Mack.

"That, Mr. Taylor, was a *very* good answer to my question."

His fingertips tickled the back of my knee and his mouth moved lazily across my shoulder. I shivered as he said, "What was the question again?" The hand on my knee trailed up the sensitive skin on the inside of my thigh. "I got distracted."

I swallowed.

We did distraction *so* well.

"I asked if you were happy."

His hand continued farther up until his touch made my back bow and my head fall back.

"Right. *That* was a stupid question."

I wanted to swat him, but I had an unsurprising lack of control over my limbs thanks to his very *focused* ministrations.

"It's not stupid," I squeezed out through clenched teeth. "I can't read your mind. Sometimes I just need to hear it."

He leaned over me, his hair mussed, but his eyes thoughtful. "And I'm bad at saying it."

"Only sometimes." Or sometimes I just needed to hear it more. I told myself that I was being stupid, but hating my insecurities didn't make them go away.

He shifted over me and settled into the crux of my thighs. Still sensitive from our last go, I whimpered when his body pressed into mine.

"In that case, you should know that every time I do this"—his hips shifted—"I am *incredibly* happy."

Somehow through all the sensation I managed to roll my eyes.

"We're talking about two different kinds of happiness."

He shook his head, and lowered his lips to my ear. "There's only one kind. Whether I'm inside you or lying beside you or touching your hair or listening to you laugh, it all means the same thing. If I'm with *you*, I'm happy."

God, he was good. At *everything*.

He hit a sensitive spot inside me, and the word *good* tumbled from my mouth by accident.

He chuckled darkly. "Are you grading me? I thought I was the teacher here."

I pulled his mouth to mine to shut him up, and then wrapped my legs around his waist.

"I'm not grading you. Your ego is big enough already."

He laughed and continued distracting me through the morning and a good portion of the afternoon.

It worked for a little while, okay maybe a long while. But when we boarded the flight late that night, no amount of flirting or touching or whispers in my ear could get my mind off the plethora of potential disasters that awaited me in London.

I knew almost nothing about his family. Except that his mother terrified me. She scared me by proxy, just based on the look on Garrick's face while he talked to her on the phone and the sound of her voice leaking from the speaker. When I saw her name on the caller ID, it was like seeing the Dark Mark hovering above my apartment.

What if she took one look at me and confirmed what I already knew to be true? Garrick was too good for me.

Don't get me wrong. I wasn't awash in self-pity about it because . . . hello, I got the guy. No complaints here. But that didn't mean I was too stupid to know that he could have someone prettier or taller or with less frizzy hair.

But he was with *me*. As long as I didn't screw it up, of course.

And God knows I was good at screwing things up.

So I sat in my seat on the plane as everyone else around me slept, including Garrick, and I drove myself crazy with worry.

If the weight of my stress were real, there was no way this plane could have stayed in the air. We'd start plummeting and spinning and then some brave soul would throw me out the side door for the good of everyone and scream, "Lighten up!" as I fell to my death.

That was *another* thing that could go wrong. I could fall to my death on the stairs at Garrick's house. Wait . . . did they have stairs? I should have made him detail it all for me. Maybe I should wake him up and ask him now about the stairs. And for a description of the entire house. And backgrounds on his parents and everyone he had ever met. Maybe he could just keep talking, so that I could stop listening to my own thoughts.

I started to reach for him, but then brought that same hand back to thump against my forehead.

Seriously, Bliss. Chill out.

That was my mantra for the rest of the trip. I repeated it in my head (and possibly out loud) as I pressed my forehead against the cool glass of the airplane window, and tried to get some sleep.

The mantra worked about as much as my attempts to sleep. Fitfully I moved between the window, the seatback tray, and Garrick's shoulder, trying to find a place to lean my head that didn't feel horrendously uncomfortable. I didn't get how I could sleep on Garrick's shoulder anytime at home, and now when it was my best option for slumber, it was like trying to rest my head on a pillow of glass shards covered in ants dusted with anthrax.

I'd switched back to the seatback tray, folding myself over onto it, when Garrick sat up and unbuckled his seat belt.

I woke him up.

Girlfriend Fail.

"I'm sorry," I whispered.

He reached between me and my current resting place, found the metal fastener of my seat belt, and clicked it open.

"What are you doing?" I asked.

He didn't even talk, just gestured with his hand for me to stand.

I fumbled to put up the tray and stand in the low space. My head craned to the side to fit under the overhead bins, and he pulled up the armrest and slid over into my spot. With his hands on my hips, he deposited me in his old seat, and then he turned toward me and leaned his back against the window. He opened his arms to me with a sleepy half smile, and I fell gratefully into his arms. With my head perched atop his chest, I sighed in relief.

"Better?" he asked, his voice raspy with sleep.

"Perfect."

His lips brushed my temple, and then sleep was almost as irresistible as he was.

I WOKE A few hours later to find light peeking through the plane windows. Two women were whispering quietly a few rows behind us in a familiar lilting accent. And it hit me. We were almost in London.

I was going to be in *London*.

God, all those months of seeing Kelsey's pictures and hearing about her travels, and I had been *raging* with jealousy. And now it was my turn.

I wanted to *mind the gap* at the tube station and eat fish and chips and try to make the Queen's guards laugh. I wanted to see Big Ben and the Globe and the London Bridge and Dame Judi Dench. Or Maggie Smith. Or Alan Rickman. Or Sir Ian McKellen. Or anybody famous and British, really.

Holy crap. This was really happening.

And I wasn't just a tourist. I was visiting with someone who'd grown up in the city. With my *fiancé*.

Take that, world.

"You look happier."

I pulled my head away from the window to find Garrick awake and staring at me. I gave a small squeal and launched myself at him. I locked our mouths together, and for a moment he sat still and shocked beneath me. Then his eyes closed, his hand cupped the back of my neck, and he kissed me so thoroughly that I almost forgot about London. *Almost.*

I broke away, grinning, and he said, "Not that I will *ever* complain about moments like that, but what's gotten into you? You waited a little late if your goal was to join the mile-high club."

I swatted his shoulder playfully, and then placed another quick kiss on his mouth because I couldn't resist. I said, "You're English."

He smiled and blinked a few times. "Yes. Yes, I am."

"And we're about to be *in* England."

He nodded slowly, and I knew I sounded crazy, but I didn't care.

"Yes. We've only been planning this visit for a month."

"I know . . . I just . . . it didn't hit me until now that we're in *London*. Or about to be, anyway. I've been worrying so much about your mother that I hadn't really thought about it. I'm going to London! Eeep!"

He chuckled, small and quiet, and brushed his fingers across my lips to quiet me. Right. People were sleeping. Then, like he couldn't contain it, he laughed louder, completely disregarding his own warning to be quiet.

"What's so funny?" I asked.

Slowly smothering his laughter, he used the hand hooked around my neck to pull my forehead against his. Our lips brushed just barely when he said, "You make me happy." I smiled my approval, and he added, "Marry me?"

My heart flip-flopped, like my unsuccessful pancakes from this morning were *supposed* to.

"You've already asked me that, and I already said yes."

"I know. It's unfair that I only get to ask you that once, though."

Melting. So much melting.

I reached up and brushed my fingertips along his jaw. He hadn't shaved in a few days, so the hair there was rough and masculine and *unbelievably* sexy. He closed his eyes and leaned into my hand the way that Hamlet did when anyone but me was playing with her. Stupid cat.

I said, "Yes. The answer will always be yes."

He took my hand from his jaw and brushed his lips across my knuckles. My insides went as gooey as the nearly congealed breakfast the flight attendants had passed out. He kissed the ring on my third finger, and who knew the engagement ring was an erogenous zone?

"I'm going to hold you to that. I know how much you love accents, and I'm going to have much more competition in that arena here."

I laughed. "I hadn't even thought of that! Just think, a whole country full of British men! I could—"

He tugged me forward and silenced me in my favorite way.

"That's not funny," he said. "It's bad enough that I'm about to have to share you with my family."

Ugh. I was going to ignore that whole family thing. I'd been enough of a Debbie Downer already to last the rest of the trip.

"Remember that time we met and you said you weren't the jealous type? Remember the time that was a big fat *lie*?"

Ah well. Jealousy looked *really* good on him.

"It wasn't a lie. I just hadn't ever met anyone worth getting jealous over until you."

I slid my arms around his waist. "Are all British men such smooth talkers?"

"No. Just me."

"And James Bond."

"Right. Of course."

"Fine. I guess since James is fictional, I'll have to keep *you*."

"You couldn't get rid of me if you tried."

"I'm *not* trying."

A flight attendant tapped me on the shoulder and asked us to please prepare for landing. I guessed what she really meant was to stop molesting my boyfriend in public.

God, airlines. Stingy with the peanuts *and* the fun.

I wasn't sorry, but I blushed anyway because that's the only thing my traitorous body was good for. I faced forward, but noticed a woman sitting across the aisle staring at us. She had her elbow on the armrest and her cheek propped up on her hand, gawking at us like we were her in-flight entertainment. My small blush spread like a wildfire across my whole face and down my neck.

Maybe we had been making a *bit* of a scene.

Garrick didn't seem to mind the attention, his chest bouncing with silent laughter. I flicked his arm, and tried to ignore the woman, who was *still* staring.

Garrick said again, "Marry me."

Oh, now he was just showing off.

I heard the woman *aww* next to us, and I swear to God I expected her to pull out a bag of popcorn or something.

I flicked his arm again, and he just laughed. I leaned my head back against the seat as the plane began to slow and dip, and I tried to get my blush under control.

Garrick stayed smug beside me as we landed and taxied

to the gate. I was glad we were near the front of the plane, so that we could grab our things and get away from our audience. I pulled my purse from under the seat in front of me, and moved to flee.

"Wait," the woman said. "Aren't you going to answer him?"

Garrick chuckled and added, "Yes, aren't you going to answer me?"

My chin dropped, and I floundered like, well, a flounder.

He was really going to make me do this with that woman watching. And now that she'd said something, a few others were paying attention, too. I pressed my lips together, and glared at him. As an actor, I *should* be better at handling attention, but it was different when I was playing a part. I got to turn off my brain and think like someone else.

Reluctantly, I said, "Yes."

"What was that, love? I couldn't quite hear you."

Cue eye roll. "I said *yes*."

Garrick turned to the people surrounding us and practically yelled, "She said yes!"

Gradually, the cabin broke out into applause, and I threw him a look that was one part I'm-going-to-murder-you and three parts get-me-out-of-here-now-kthxbye.

Garrick soaked up the applause with a charming smile while I looked on, probably barely more attractive than a radish. I turned to flee and tripped over something. I couldn't actually see anything, but I *swear* there was something.

I power-walked off the plane and resisted the urge to run down the walkway and into the terminal. Garrick caught up to me just as I passed through the door, and looped an arm around my neck.

"You know I love it when you blush."

"And you know I hate it."

"It reminds me of your face the second time we met, that morning in my classroom. The most inappropriate time and place to ever be turned on, but you've got a take-no-prisoners kind of blush. My body didn't give me much of a choice."

He was only saying that to make me blush more. You would think that I'd be a bit more comfortable talking about sex, now that I'd had it and all. You would also think that at my age I would be able to successfully insert the straw into a Capri Sun juice pouch. I was 0–2 there.

So I let him enjoy my embarrassment. And I enjoyed the way his side was pressed against mine. Fair trade.

3

Garrick

I WAS STILL a bit bleary-eyed as we waited through the long line for immigration, then picked up our bags, and passed through customs. Bliss vaulted between exuberance and silence, more of the latter, as we got closer to our final destination.

Outside the airport, I tucked Bliss under my arm, needing to feel her, to feel some sort of control as her panic began to bleed into me. I was halfheartedly trying to flag down a taxi to take us to my parents' place in Kensington when I heard someone shout, "Taylor! Garrick Taylor! Look over here, you prat!"

Bliss had already stopped and was staring at two idiots down the pavement, yelling and waving their arms. The first idiot had dark skin and a buzzed head that had been covered in dreads the last time I'd seen him. That would be Rowland. And paired with the second idiot, Graham, who looked enough like me to pass for my brother (a scam we'd used more than once when we were kids), they meant trouble.

I passed a hand through my hair and smiled. "Bloody hell."

What in the world were they doing here?

"Friends of yours?" Bliss asked.

"Very old friends."

Bliss and I turned around our luggage and barely made it a few meters before Rowland was tackling me.

"Ricky!" he yelled, messing with my hair.

I heard Bliss say, "Ricky?" over my shoulder before I shoved Rowland off. Glaring, I said, "That nickname wasn't okay in secondary, and it isn't okay now."

Graham said, "Oh, come on, brother. At least let him have a little fun. You've not visited in ages. Though I can see why."

I didn't have to look to know he was staring at Bliss. Not only did Graham and I look alike—tall, blond hair, blue eyes—but we had the same taste in women. I had mostly been joking with her earlier about finding another guy, but now it wasn't so funny. I shook my head at him and pulled her closer to me.

"Bliss, these two gits are my old mates, Rowland and Graham. We came up together. And this is my fiancée, Bliss."

God, it felt good saying that.

"Her name is Bliss? Or is that your nickname for her because she's really good in—"

"Rowland," I warned.

He shrugged and shot Bliss a cheeky smile. She was grinning at both of them, her cheeks a brilliant red. And as good as it was to see them, I was not even remotely keen on sharing her.

I asked, "What are you lot doing here?"

Rowland said, "We phoned your dad and told him to tell your mum that your flight had been delayed by a few hours."

"Why would you do that?"

Graham grinned in Bliss's direction and said, "Because we wanted to meet your girl . . . before your mum tore her to pieces."

I saw the blood drain from her face, and she went from red to white in seconds. Well, there went the last of her calm.

"Garrick!" Her hand connected with my arm, and then again with my chest.

Throwing a glare at Graham, I caught her hands and pulled her close.

"He's joking, love. It's all going to be fine."

Please let it be fine.

"Or after a few pints with us, it will be, anyway," Rowland cut in.

"It's the middle of the day," I said.

Rowland shrugged. "We'll make sure there's some food had somewhere in there."

Bliss had her arms crossed over her chest, glaring at me. She looked so bloody hot when she was angry that I almost didn't mind.

I said, "Thank you both for coming. And for managing to piss my future bride off in record time. But it was a long flight. I should probably just get Bliss home."

When I reached, her hand flitted out of my range and then came back to poke me in the chest. "Oh no you don't, Mr. Taylor." I heard Rowland laugh behind me. She continued, "You are not depriving me of the chance to gather some much needed liquid courage or to question your friends."

Graham whistled. "I like this one."

That much was uncomfortably clear.

I met her eyes, and she wasn't backing down. I pressed my lips together into a thin line, but her eyebrows just rose in answer.

"Fine. Okay." I turned to my old friends and added, "One drink. With food. One hour. That's it." They held up innocent hands in surrender, and started leading us down the pavement.

Over his shoulder, Graham said, "Damn, Taylor. Did teaching suck all the fun out of you?"

"Something got sucked while he was teaching."

I shoved Rowland from behind, and he launched forward several feet, cackling.

"What?" Bliss asked. "What did he say?"

"Nothing. Just being a prick."

Rowland kept his distance as he led us to the same old Peugeot he'd been driving the last time I'd lived in London nearly eight years ago. It was funny how little some things and some people changed.

I'd changed . . . that much was for sure. In turns, I'd been just as elitist and judgmental as my parents or I'd rebelled and battled that with tremendous levels of stupidity and trouble. It was only in the last two years that I'd started to feel like I'd finally found a reasonable middle ground. I could only pray to find something similar today with my parents. I could only pray that this whole trip wouldn't blow up in my face.

I helped Bliss into the backseat, and then turned to Graham before sliding in after her. He didn't just look like a brother to me; he'd felt like one for most of my life, too. And when I left this city, I'd left that friendship, too. I'd only just recently reached out to him to reconnect.

I said, "It's really good to see you, mate. Sorry that I've done a botch job of keeping in touch."

He clapped me on the back and shook his head. "Don't worry about it. I get why you stayed away. And things seemed to have worked themselves out just fine." I peeked into the car, where Bliss was smiling and listening to some no doubt filthy story that Rowland was telling her from the driver's seat. I smiled. "Yeah, things have worked out perfectly."

I climbed into the backseat and pulled Bliss over to meet me in the middle. My old mates might have been troublemakers of the highest order, but they did have one thing going for them; Bliss was the most relaxed I'd seen her in the last week.

Maybe it was a good idea to just let loose for a little while. We both needed it.

I brought her head close to mine, pressing my nose into her curls as she laughed at the ridiculous voice Rowland was doing in imitation of his mother. Her warmth, her scent calmed me. And she made me see London in a new light. She made me see it how it was before my parents and all their pressure and manipulation had made me want to leave.

Again and again, Bliss seemed to be my new beginning, the thing to help me let go of the past and move forward.

She rested a hand on my thigh and looked up at me. I must have been tuned out for longer than I realized because she asked, "You okay?"

I laid my hand over hers and said, "Just glad to be home and to have you with me."

She turned her hand over and laced her fingers with mine, and Rowland made gagging noises in the front seat.

"Oh shut it, Row. You're just jealous because you haven't yet managed to hold on to a woman for more than one night."

"Managed? *Managed?* I should win an award for that. It's harder than you think."

Bliss snuggled into my side and asked, "So how long have you known Garrick?"

Rowland answered, "I've only known him since secondary."

"High school," I translated for Bliss.

"But Graham and Garrick have been attached at the hip since they were in nappies."

"Diapers," I added.

"Hey, she gets the gist of it. No need to translate every bleeding thing I say. I'm speaking English."

"So what you're saying," Bliss began, leaning forward between the two front seats, "is that Graham is the one to go to for the embarrassing stories?"

"Excuse me." I poked her in the side, and she squirmed away from me.

"Oh come on. Like you don't know enough embarrassing things about me. You've been there for too many of them."

"Do tell," Rowland said, his eyebrows waggling at us through the rearview mirror.

"Don't. You. Dare." It was her turn to poke me.

"Wait." Graham turned in his seat to face us. "Are you talking about being all hot for teacher?"

"Garrick!" I had a feeling I was going to be hearing my name in that tone all too often on this trip. "You told them?"

"I told Graham. Since Rowland doesn't seem too surprised, I'm guessing he's been filled in."

Bliss bent and buried her face in her hands. "Oh my God, I'm so embarrassed."

"Why would you be embarrassed?" Rowland asked.

"You can't get much hotter than a schoolgirl fantasy. After Graham told me, I had dreams for a week featuring girls in our old school uniforms."

Bliss gave a garbled groan and sank even further until her face rested against her knees. I was still learning the intricacies of speaking Bliss, but I was fairly certain that groan meant that she thought she was dying of mortification.

I leveled a stare at him and said, "Thanks a lot, mate."

Then I ran a hand across the curve of Bliss's back and said, "There's no reason to be embarrassed, because we didn't do anything wrong. I don't ever want to have to lie about us again."

Call it an issue. Call it baggage. But I really hated lies. They're ugly things, festering like wounds, spreading like disease. They're winner-less crimes that hurt everybody in the end.

I felt her back rise and fall in a heaving breath beneath my hand. "You're right." She sat up, and I kept my hand between her and the seat. "I'm not sorry, and I'm done being scared of it."

"Thatta girl," Rowland said.

"That's *my* girl," I said into her ear.

"You hold on to that thick skin, sweetheart. Let Graham and I treat you to a few pints and you'll have armor by the time you're standing in the Taylors' grand foyer."

"You have a grand foyer?" She paled.

I scratched at my neck and said, "It's really only slightly grand."

"What about stairs? Do you have stairs?"

I nodded.

She threw her hands up. "That's it. I'm gonna die. I knew it."

I saw Rowland and Graham glance at each other in confusion, then look at me. I shook my head because I had no idea. Maybe I could be a bit lenient about that one-drink rule.

"I don't know what you're talking about, but you're not going to die. It's just a house. Nothing to worry about."

It really was just a house. I'd not ever really thought of it as a home.

She took a breath and nodded. Sitting up taller, she gave me a determined look.

Stairs. Cats. I loved the woman, but God knows I didn't always understand her. She was so afraid of little things— mothers and fancy houses—but when she set her mind to something, she tackled it with such ferocity. Big things. Scary things.

Her career in Philly. Life after college. Falling in love with me.

I was the one that struggled with the big picture. I never quite knew what I wanted until it had already slapped me around a bit.

Or until she walked into my life with an imaginary cat.

"SHE DOESN'T NEED another one, Rowland. She's good."

We were both good. If I drank any more, I wouldn't

have a filter by the time we met my parents, which was a bit like not having a life raft on the *Titanic*.

"Oh, come on. What's the point of working in a pub if I can't get my friends completely sloshed?"

There was something terribly wrong about being in a near-empty pub midday and having as much alcohol as we had.

"I don't know . . . gainful employment? Saving up to finally stop living with your parents?"

"Ssh!" He waved a forceful hand at me, like the two people in a booth across the bar were going to hear.

"First of all, that was cold, mate. And second, I have my own flat. It just *happens* to be above my parents' garage. That doesn't count as living with my parents."

"Whatever helps you sleep at night, Row."

"Just for that . . ." He poured another glass and slid it in Bliss's direction.

I snatched it away as she reached for it, and pulled it away from her.

"Hey!" Her bottom lip curled into a pout. An *almost* irresistible pout.

"Sweetheart, I think you're fine without it."

She teetered toward me on her stool, wrapping a hand around my neck. Her fingers tangled in the hair at the base of my neck and she said, "Well, if I can't have it, you should drink it."

Rowland cut in, "Now, *that* is a plan. Maybe another drink will make you less of a bore."

"I'm not boring."

Graham gave a loud snore, pretending to sleep with his head balanced on the top of his mug.

Bliss laughed raucously, and the only thing that kept her from toppling off her seat was my hand at her waist. Graham's eyes opened, and he winked at her before giving another overdramatic snore.

That did it.

I took hold of Bliss's stool and dragged it over right next to mine. She squealed and fell into me. I tried to not to look too obviously annoyed at Graham as I draped my arm over her shoulder and took a swig of beer.

Rowland cheered, Bliss hummed against the skin of my neck, and I told myself one drink wouldn't hurt.

Famous last words.

4

Bliss

"OKAY, NOW WE'RE really done," Garrick said, his voice deep and hypnotic.

I didn't want to be done. This was so much more fun than meeting his parents. I rested my chin on his shoulder and said, "Just one more."

He glanced down at me and said, "Trust me, love. You're going to want to stop now. Otherwise you'll be making up songs and talking about how good I smell and getting inappropriately touchy."

I laid my cheek down on his shoulder and slipped my fingers just below the collar of his shirt. "I thought you liked it when I was inappropriately touchy."

Garrick stilled my hand at his neck and said, "Not when we're about to meet my mother."

Oh God. His mother. It shouldn't be funny, but I found myself laughing anyway. I had to laugh . . . or I might cry. I know he said that Rowland and Graham were joking, but I was fairly certain he was just trying to keep me from running.

Rowland said, "Your mum will understand. The two of you are practically on a honeymoon already. It's pretty nauseating."

Graham added, "Of course she'll understand. I mean, she's your mom. It's not like she hasn't had sex before."

Oh God. Now I was going to laugh *and* cry.

Graham leaned around me to look at Garrick, whose face was scrunched up in possibly the only unattractive expression I had ever seen on his face. Taunting Garrick further, he said, "I bet your parents are doing it right now. Sneaking in a quick shag while your flight is 'delayed.' "

Garrick slid off his stool. "And . . . that's our cue to call it a night."

"And call a therapist." Graham smiled.

"And get coffee," I added. Definitely coffee.

Garrick stood behind me, and his warm hands gripped my shoulders. I leaned back and tilted my head until my head rested against his stomach, and I was looking at him upside down. I blinked. Or I meant to, anyway. Instead, my eyes stayed closed, and the dark swirled with color, and I had the sensation that I was tumbling down a long black hole. I peeled my lids open, and then had to squint against the light of the bar. Between being upside down and being two drinks past the point of caring, the world was horrendously disoriented. "I *think* . . ." I looked up at Garrick. "That I drank too much."

Garrick nodded, and if his heavy-lidded eyes were any indication, he wasn't exactly sober, either. Or he was turned on. Or both . . . hopefully.

He said, "*I think* I'm friends with a couple pricks."

Graham stood, leaving his half-empty beer on the bar. "Take it easy on the mushy stuff, Taylor. We know how much you love us. No need to make a spectacle."

"Let's just get out of here," Garrick said.

I agreed by looping my arms around his waist and laying my head against his chest.

Rowland said, "At least she's relaxed now. I did you a favor."

I was gloriously relaxed, in fact. And I figured . . . maybe we could stretch out this fake plane delay for a little longer, get a little time on our own in the city before I had to walk the plank. I slid my hands down to the leather belt that wrapped around his hips, and lifted up on my tiptoes. Humming, I found the warm crux where the muscles of his shoulder flowed into his neck. This was the perfect part of him. When I took a deep breath, I could almost imagine we were alone, and I was surrounded by him.

Garrick cleared his throat. "Maybe a little too relaxed."

I opened my lips and tasted perfection, too. A small noise of satisfaction rolled from my lips, and somewhere behind me I heard, "Rowland really *did* do you a favor."

Gently, Garrick pushed me down until my feet were flat on the ground, and I could no longer reach his neck.

He held up his middle finger toward his friends. Graham raised his eyebrows, and Garrick seemed to realize we weren't in the States anymore. He blinked and shook his head, and then added a second finger. It looked like a backward peace sign, but I knew it didn't mean that. Not here.

Graham shook his head. "Damn it. The Americans got to you."

Garrick flipped him off with two fingers again, this time with a bit more conviction. I watched on, only vaguely aware of what was happening, until the both of them burst into laughter.

I rolled my eyes.

Men.

Garrick kept a tight hold on my hand as we left the pub, and then we headed back to the car we'd arrived in. Garrick lowered me into the backseat first, and then climbed in after me.

I neglected the seat belt in favor of wrapping myself around Garrick. I found that spot on his neck again and sighed. "You really do smell *so* good."

He laughed. "You always say that, especially when you've been drinking."

That's because it was true. I'd never really gotten scent as a turn-on. When I'd bought cologne for previous boyfriends, it kind of all smelled the same to me. I usually made someone in the store pick for me. But with Garrick . . . God, I just wanted to be surrounded by his smell all the time. If I couldn't be near him, I wanted to wear his clothes or sleep on his side of the bed.

I was a creeper. I could accept that.

Maybe it was the alcohol or being in a foreign city or the fact that this was the first time we'd really been out drinking together since the night we met; Whatever it was, I wanted him, so bad that my skin itched to touch his. I fiddled with one of the buttons on his shirt, trying to act as innocent as possible. And then ever so slowly, I slipped his top button open. His head didn't move, so I went for a second button.

Apparently one button was my stealth limit because he totally caught me. I smiled up at him as sweetly as I could and slid my fingers under his shirt to the bare skin of his chest. His chin dipped, and he stared at me in warning, but he didn't stop me. I trailed my fingers across his collarbone and from his shoulder back down to his chest. He watched me with dark eyes, and the arm draped over the seat behind me came down around me. His fingertips slid under my shirt to curve over my shoulder.

Shifting, I faced him, leaning my other shoulder against the seat and draping my legs over his lap. Immediately, his other hand curved around my calf.

I might be clueless about a lot of things, but I knew my fiancé. He was definitely a leg man.

Between his touch and the alcohol, I felt light-headed.

That *might* have been mostly the alcohol, considering how heavy my head felt and the way the world in my peripheral vision kept swooping and spinning. His fingertips found the back of my knee, and I giggled at his touch.

"Aw, man." Rowland said from the front. "You two are like a bunch of randy teenagers."

I felt like a teenager. I hadn't been this drunk in ages. I was too busy working and working and then working some more.

Being an adult blows.

I tilted my head up to Garrick and said, "I can't feel my lips."

"Here, let me check." His mouth slanted over mine, his tongue dipping between my lips, tangling with mine. He tasted like beer and himself, and I realized that he'd had almost as much to drink as me. He pulled back. "Nope, they're still there."

He grinned playfully, and that was when I knew he'd had *plenty* to drink. Laughing, I hooked my arms around his neck, and lay back against the seat cushion, pulling him with me.

"Hey, hey now!" Rowland called. "No sex while I'm driving. That's a public hazard."

Garrick's lips ran down my neck, and I couldn't seem to make myself stop giggling. I called back to Rowland, "So pull over."

"Are you seriously going to have sex in my car? Because that's hot. Can she be on top?"

Garrick said, "Eyes on the road, Rowland! No one is having sex."

I frowned, and he kissed my puckered bottom lip. He muttered, "*You* are a public hazard."

Graham leaned around his seat to look at us. "You two don't need coffee. You need a fucking tranquilizer."

Groaning, Garrick's hands slipped off my body to brace against the seat. He pushed himself back into a sitting position, and I whined at the distance.

Whined. I would have been embarrassed if I wasn't so turned on.

He clenched his fists and tilted his head back against the seat.

Of all the times for him to practice restraint. I was going to burn up in my skin here.

Staring up at the ceiling, he spoke, his voice strained. "Sorry about that."

"Sorry?" I asked. "Who's sorry?"

"I'm not!" Rowland said.

I trailed my fingers over his arm. "I'm sorry you stopped."

Garrick glared at Rowland in the rearview mirror until his eyes focused back on the road. Then he turned to me and pointed at his friend. "*That's* why I'm sorry."

Somewhere in my body, I was fairly certain I still had a brain. And it had probably been shouting at me for a while. But my hormones must have had fucking megaphones because that's all I could hear. I sat up, my arms and legs shaky with pent-up need. My shirt was twisted, and you could see the blue lace of my bra and the swell of my chest peeking out from the neckline of my shirt. I adjusted it quickly, glancing to see if Rowland or Graham had seen, but luckily they were still looking ahead. My eyes skipped to Garrick's dark gaze. Yeah, he definitely hadn't missed it.

A bolt of electricity shot through me, and I pressed my thighs together, trying to relieve something, *anything*. Garrick leaned over and his lips brushed my ear. *So* not helping the situation. As I tried to keep from squirming, he said, "As much as I'm dying to have you right now, you're mine. And I don't share."

I swallowed, and squeezed my legs tighter. This was somehow the worst and best moment of my life. In fact, most of our relationship fell into those categories. Best boyfriend. Worst embarrassing moment. Best kiss. Worst excuse ever. Best (well . . . only) sex. Worst timing. But I could take all the worsts, if the best always followed.

His nose brushed my jaw and his breath fanned across my neck, and I swear my body shook in response. You would think with the morning he'd spent distracting me before our flight, I wouldn't be so desperate for him now, but I was always desperate for him.

Plus, even though we lived together, I never saw him enough. Between plays and the additional jobs it took to pay our rent in Center City, it felt like we were always on the go. I couldn't remember the last time we'd gone out for a night together, at least not when we hadn't just finished a show and weren't exhausted.

All those years of making up excuses not to have sex, and now I was busy trying to think of an excuse to ditch his friends and his parents and keep him all to myself.

His lips brushed against my ear again, and I dropped

a hand to his thigh and squeezed. I wasn't sure whether I was signaling him to stop or to give me more; I just knew I was *dying* from his proximity alone. A low rumble spilled from his throat, and I glanced up front to make sure his friends weren't watching. They weren't, so I took a chance and slid my hand a little higher.

I didn't get but an inch before his hand clamped down on mine. Against my ear, he growled, "You really are a hazard to my health." I just squeezed his leg again, and leaned my head to offer him more of my neck. He nipped my skin there and then whispered, "We're going to meet my parents. We'll smile and talk long enough that they feel like they've met you, then we're finding a place to be alone. My bedroom, the bathroom, the kitchen, I don't care where. The only thing I care about is fucking you so hard you can't see straight."

Annnd . . . aneurysm.

The air fled my lungs like I'd been punched in the chest, and I blushed so hard I felt like my blood was boiling. Seriously. It had turned so hot in this backseat, I was going to have a freaking heatstroke. And I had to bite down hard on my lip to keep in the string of unintelligible noises building on my tongue.

Garrick and I had sex. Often. *Good* sex. But in the spectrum of intercourse (oh God, only my brain would think *spectrum of intercourse* at a time like this), we made love. It was intense and sweet and perfect. I don't know if it was the alcohol or my actions that pushed him to the other side of the spectrum, but I knew I was wound tight enough that another minute of him whispering in my ear could probably send me over the edge. That was probably why my arms and legs felt like Jell-O when we stood in front of his parents' door, and he rang the bell. Though I'm sure the alcohol and the stress and the traveling didn't help.

"This is going to be okay, right?" I asked. "You can't tell I'm drunk, right?"

And would his parents be able to tell that I'd just been dying to screw their son in the backseat of a car like a high school prom date? That I was *still* dying to?

I could picture it now.

Hi Mom and Dad, this is my girlfriend—

HARLOT!

Then they would make me sew a red *A* on all of my clothing, and I did *not* look good in red, what with all the blushing. Plus I'd barely passed my costuming class in college. Needles and me don't mix.

A hand came down on my shoulder, and I jumped. Rowland smiled, "You're good, Bliss. You're going to be a smash. Just wait."

Right. I was going to be fine.

Garrick rang the doorbell a second time, and when no one answered, Graham said, "Told you they were shagging."

Throwing a glare over his shoulder, Garrick took a deep breath and squared his shoulders. I stared, and for the first time realized that he was as nervous as I was. Oh hell, if he was nervous I was doomed. My odds were looking about as good as a main character in *Game of Thrones*.

He turned the knob. It gave way in his hand, and the

door swung open to reveal a darkened entryway. My footsteps echoed as we stepped inside.

"That's strange," he said, his voice echoing, too.

Did this mean we could just go straight to his bedroom? Because oh my yes, thank you.

The open door let in just enough late afternoon light to reveal a strip of empty . . . well, foyer. Never thought I would have the need to actually use that word in real life. The windows were covered by heavy curtains, draping the rest of the place in darkness. I reached for the wall beside the door, running my hands along it looking for a switch.

I wasn't sure which of my many issues to blame when my forearm collided with something cool and smooth and vase-shaped, knocking it sideways. When I tried to catch it and missed, I was blaming my sex-distracted thoughts. When I heard it crash and shatter against the floor, I was blaming the alcohol. When the light flipped on revealing a *seriously* grand foyer, a large group of people streaming into the entryway holding champagne flutes, and an elegant and terrifying woman that could only be Garrick's mother staring in horror . . . well, that's when I knew it wasn't any of those things.

It was just me . . . failing at life again.

Behind me, Rowland broke the silence with a tentative "Surprise?"

No . . . me being a disaster of awkward proportions was the least surprising thing ever. I'd made a smash all right. Like I was the Hulk's cousin.

Bliss SMASH.

5

Garrick

THE CRASH OF the vase echoed through the foyer for several seconds afterward, and each reverberation seemed to cause my mother's expression to contort further.

I'd always thought I was fairly good at thinking on my feet and reacting in a crisis (and looking at my mother, this definitely counted as a crisis). For the life of me though, I couldn't think of a single thing to say. Maybe I was out of practice or maybe there still wasn't enough blood flowing through my brain, but either way only one word was going through my mind.

Fuck.

And not the kind I'd had in mind.

Luckily, my father, ever the composed businessman, covered for us all.

"Well . . . wasn't that quite the entrance?"

The crowd laughed, and I could almost feel the heat of Bliss's blush from here. The entire downstairs was brimming with what seemed like every person I had ever met, and plenty that I hadn't. And I hadn't the foggiest clue about what they were doing here.

Dad crossed to Bliss, and she looked queasy enough to pass out. He was immaculate in a dark suit that contrasted with his silvering hair. He picked up her hand and kissed the back of it. Her eyes flicked to mine, surprised.

Dad said, his voice loud enough for everyone to hear, "Don't you worry about it for one second, sweetheart. I'm sure at some point in his life Garrick had already broken that old thing and glued it back together."

Mum would have flayed me. She loved that vase. But the people laughed, and the room collectively sighed in relief. Dad was good at that kind of stuff. He could charm any conference room, any party, any seminar. It was the one-on-one things he couldn't do.

Dad helped Bliss step over the glass shards, and that made me spring into action. We crossed to each other, but Dad stayed in between us. Still holding one of her hands, he clapped me on the shoulder and looked out at the crowd.

"Well, we wanted a surprise engagement party, and we certainly got a surprise." Everyone laughed again. Dad squeezed my shoulder and said, "You all know my son, Garrick." I spotted a few business types in the crowd—salt and pepper hair, pristine suits, impeccable ties. I sure as hell didn't know *them*. Mixing business with family as always.

"He graduated at the top of his class, and his mother and I were ready for him to go to Oxford like all the other Taylor men." Here we go. Time for the not-so-sly insults about how I'd ruined our family legacy. "But children have to make their own way, or they'll only pretend to grow up. I'm proud to look at him and see the man he has become."

I tried not to gape. My mother and I spoke often enough, but I couldn't even recall the last time Dad and I had actually spoken. He'd been furious when I left, and certain that I'd ruined my life. Was it possible that my parents had done some changing of their own? This new leaf threw me off balance, and suddenly all I could think about was the scent of beer on my breath and how disheveled I probably looked. "He left us to make his own way and moved to America, where he's already managed to become a university professor at his young age."

Okay, so his storytelling was a bit selective considering I was no longer a professor. But it was a compliment nonetheless.

"He's become a fine man and has now brought home this lovely, unpredictable young woman to join our family." He turned to Bliss, holding up her hand. "We're so happy to have you here, Bliss." Then he turned out to the crowd. "We're happy to have *all* of you here to celebrate their engagement with us. Please, eat, drink, enjoy yourselves. Though perhaps keep an eye on the decor." He winked, and Bliss laughed, completely charmed.

He presented her hand to me as people around the house clapped, and then without actually saying a private word to either of us, retreated to a group of men in suits.

I wanted to punch myself. People laughed and *aww*'d at his performance, and I'd been sucked in just like the rest of them. Like I was sixteen all over again, I churned with rage and wanted to storm out of the door.

So much for that new leaf.

He'd thrown this stupid party to impress people, and he'd made it a surprise so that I couldn't object. Just once I would love to see my father try to do something important without an audience.

I schooled my face into a blank expression, and then concentrated on Bliss. I placed a kiss on her temple. She hugged me, and against my chest, I heard her say, "Kill me. Just put me out of my misery, please."

"And leave me to be miserable without you? Never."

"So selfish."

"When it comes to you? Absolutely." Already I wanted to just take her away, to just be the two of us again. I sighed and looked around. Some people were staying in the foyer, others were streaming into other parts of the house, laughing and drinking, and grabbing hors d'oeuvres from passing waiters.

I said, "I guess our odds of finding somewhere to be alone just got significantly smaller."

She looked up at me and frowned. She looked so disappointed that my stomach clenched with desire all over again.

Just a few hours. This thing couldn't last forever.

"I'm so sorry about the vase. And for making such a scene." Her face scrunched up like she was going to cry, and my method of dealing with her tears yesterday morning probably wasn't going to fly in this room full of people. I smoothed a hand over her hair and said the only thing I could.

"Marry me?"

Her eyes turned sad.

"Garrick, not now."

My heart twisted. It was another one of those moments. "Yes, now, love. Marry me."

"Still? You know I'm just going to keep breaking things."

"And you know I'm just going to keep loving you anyway." Her frown twitched, and I added, "Besides . . . not marrying you would break *me*."

The frown softened, and she blinked away the film of tears in her eyes. "Me too."

"It's settled then. You're stuck with me forever."

She shook her head and made a noise that sounded like disbelief.

My biggest fear was that someday she would talk herself out of our relationship. That she would shake her head and listen more to her own poisonous thoughts than the words coming out of my mouth.

I kissed her cheek and whispered in her ear, "We *are* forever. If you don't believe me, I'll have to make you. As soon as we find that place to be alone."

I only got a faint pink in her cheeks as she looked down at her feet, but I'd take it. After a second, she tipped her head back and groaned, a sound that went straight through me.

She said, "I'm wearing *jeans*."

I nodded. I loved those jeans. They fit her perfectly.

"And by the looks of it, I'm in a room filled with people in designer dresses. And you're crazy if you think this foyer is only *slightly* grand. There's a freaking chandelier."

"Luckily that can't be knocked over." Mum's voice was like whiskey, it came off smooth, but ended with a burn.

"Mum." It was halfway between a greeting and a warning.

"Hi sweetheart." She leaned up and kissed my cheek before turning to Bliss.

"Mum, this is Bliss. Bliss, my mother."

She smiled. "What a name."

Bliss knotted her fingers together. "Um . . . thank you?"

Mum's smile was all red lips, white teeth, and sugared kindness. It was the razor-sharp tongue behind those teeth that I was worried about.

"Mrs. Taylor," Bliss began. "I am so sorry about the vase. I don't even know how to begin apologizing."

"Then don't." God, my mother's voice should be listed on WebMD as a cause of frostbite. "It was just an accident after all."

"I am so very sorry though. And so thankful that you've welcomed me into your home. It's so nice to meet you. And I'm just so, so happy to be here."

"*So* you are. And we're happy that our Garrick has come home. And brought you along, of course."

"Yes, I'm so happy to be here."

"You've already said that much." She turned to me then. "She's very sweet, Garrick. Is it just the clumsiness she's overcompensating for? Or something worse?"

And so it began.

I laughed like she was joking. Because that's how you have to handle my mother. She wants a reaction, and humor is the safest one. I kept laughing, and after a few moments, Bliss's uneasy laugh joined mine.

I changed the subject before Mum could point out that she wasn't, in fact, joking.

"Was this party your idea, Mother?"

She gave me a look before rolling her eyes toward Dad. "Your father wanted to make sure you and your fiancée had the best welcome possible."

Read: He wanted to take advantage of the opportunity to show off. The "best welcome" was just the company line. And though my mother certainly had her issues, I loved her for not even pretending to go along with it.

"Right. Thanks for *that*."

She gave a single, solitary chuckle and took a long drink from her champagne. Mum *hated* events like this. I suppose that was at least one thing that she and Bliss had in common.

I saw Bliss fidgeting with her shirt and shifting her feet.

"Mum, would you excuse us for a moment? Since we

had no warning, we're not quite dressed for a party. We'll get changed and then come back down."

"Of course, dear. That's definitely a good idea. Just casual party attire will do fine."

As we turned to grab our luggage, Bliss said, "In what world is *this* casual?"

My world, unfortunately. Or my old one anyway.

I took her bag for her, and said, "We're upstairs. I'm right behind you."

I didn't have to tell her twice. At the speed she went, I'm sure she was tempted to take it two stairs at a time.

I directed her toward my old room. She breezed through the door, and didn't stop until she had thrown herself facedown on the bed with a groan.

"I'm never going back out there. I'll climb out the window."

I parked our luggage just inside the room, and then shut the door behind me. I took a seat beside her and laid a hand on her back. "Look on the bright side, we've got some alone time after all."

She rolled over, putting herself farther away from me.

"Sorry, but I'm not exactly in the mood anymore."

I winced.

"Bliss, I—"

She pushed herself up and off the bed and began pacing. "Why couldn't you just tell me that she was going to hate me? Why tell me again and again that I was worrying over nothing when I clearly *wasn't*?"

"I didn't want you to worry. I thought things would go smoother if you were calm."

"Have you met me? Smooth is not an option I come with. If you're looking for smooth, maybe you should look elsewhere."

Mid-pace, I caught her by the elbows and made her face me.

"Don't do that. Don't push me away."

She covered her hands with her hands and took a deep breath. "I'm sorry. I didn't mean that. I just . . . I didn't expect it to be like *this*."

"What does that mean?"

She shook her head, and dropped her hands to look up at the ceiling instead. "Nothing. It's . . . nothing."

She pulled away and went to her suitcase. She went to put it up on the bed, took a long look at the white bedding, and then laid it on the floor.

"Bliss, talk to me."

"Do you think this is okay? It's the best I have." She stood, pulling a simple blue cotton dress from her bag.

"Bliss, you can wear whatever you want down there. I only said we were going to change to give us a break."

"Right. Maybe I can find some decent jewelry. Just give me a couple minutes." She took the dress and a few other items, and disappeared into the bathroom. The door closed behind her with a click, and it was my turn to throw myself back on my bed.

I stared up at the ceiling and cursed under my breath.

Maybe my fears were warranted after all.

6

Bliss

THIS WAS A joke. A massively unfunny joke.

I'd fixed my hair, retouched my makeup, donned my best outfit, thrown on my best jewelry, and I was fairly certain that their toilet bowl scrubber still cost more than my entire outfit.

Why hadn't he told me?

I got that he didn't talk about his family much. They clearly weren't close. God knows I didn't talk about mine much, either, except to complain. But you'd think he could have just taken half a second to drop a quick "By the way, my family is loaded" into conversation.

If I was worried that Mrs. Taylor *might* think I wasn't good enough for her son before, it was pretty much a so-lidified fact now.

I didn't fit here. At all. Not even almost. One of these things is *really* not like the others.

And to make matters worse, Garrick looked perfect when I exited the bathroom. He'd donned a button-up shirt and tie to go with his khaki pants, and he looked effortless. Unlike me, he fit.

And a small, niggling voice in my mind asked how it was possible then that we fitted together? I shook my head to clear my thoughts, and Garrick crossed the room to place a kiss on my forehead.

"You look lovely."

I smiled, but I didn't feel it. "Thanks. So do you."

"Everything is going to be fine."

He'd said that so many times that it didn't mean anything anymore. Like when you say a word too much and it stops sounding like itself and feels alien and foreign in your head.

"Let's go then," I said.

His hands cupped my jaw, and he leaned in for a kiss. I tilted my head back away from him.

"You'll get lipstick on you."

"I don't care, love. The only thing I care about right now in this entire house is you."

My resolve melted, and he brushed a feather-light kiss across my lips, somehow coming out lipstick-free. He laced our fingers together and planted another kiss on the back of my hand.

I wanted the gesture to be comforting, but it only made me more unsettled. It only made me wonder more what he could *possibly* see in me.

Together, we descended the stairs back into the jungle of champagne flutes and designer handbags and outfits that put mine to shame. It was a forest of self-esteem issues waiting to happen, and I was smack-dab in the middle of it.

We'd barely made it two feet past the base of the stairs before we were intercepted by a group of people.

"Garrick! So good to see you!"

He let go of my hand to greet a guy about Garrick's age. He had dark hair, combed perfectly, and wore a suit. Again, I say, in what world is a *suit* casual?

"John, it's good to see you, too. This is my fiancée, Bliss."

John turned to the side and a woman stepped up beside him. She, too, had dark hair, fixed into a perfect bun at the nape of her neck. I concentrated on not touching my out-of-control curls in response.

"Lovely to meet you, Bliss. This is my wife, Amy."

I smiled. "It's nice to meet you."

God, this was repetitive.

She laughed. "Oh no, the pleasure is all mine."

I was probably supposed to say something more, but all that came to mind was insisting that the pleasure was actually mine, like a freaking tug of war. But that would have been a lie anyway, so I just stayed silent.

After a few painful seconds, Garrick added, "John and I went to school together."

John nodded, his smile plastic. "I loved your father's reminder that you were first in our class. Still can't get away from coming in second even all these years later."

Garrick laughed, and I could tell he was uncomfortable by the stiffness of his hand when he laced our fingers together again. But you would never know it from his face.

Maybe that's what I needed to do to get through this. I needed to act. I needed to turn off Bliss and become someone else, someone who fit in this place and knew what to say and what *not* to say. If I became that someone else, I could separate my thoughts from my own worries and maybe get through this night intact. The stage was the only place I ever really felt confident, and I could use a bit of confidence at the moment. So that's what I did. I played a part.

"So John," I asked. "What have you been doing since the last time you and Garrick saw each other? Catch us up."

"Well"—he kissed the back of Amy's hand—"I got married. Beat you on that front, at least." God, this guy was a prick. No wonder Garrick was so stiff. "I'm now working as a software designer."

"A software designer? That's interesting. I bet that's challenging."

"Oh, not really. It's a bit boring really. Though I'm sure in comparison to what Taylor over here is doing these days, it probably looks like brain surgery."

I laughed, thinking with each little chuckle how satisfying it would be to punch him in the face.

"Well, some of us are blessed to have careers that we love and are simple *because* we love them. Others get jobs that are, what did you say? Boring? But maybe someday you'll grow to love it."

Garrick lowered his head and gave a cough that was

suspiciously laugh-like and said, "It's was nice chatting with you John, Amy. But we should probably make the rounds. Lots of people to see."

Once he'd led me a few feet away, his shoulders began to bounce in laughter.

He said, "I realize I'm being redundant now, but I just can't help it. Marry me?"

"You're going to make me wear out the word *yes*."

"Nah. I'm saving that goal for our wedding night."

Miraculously, I managed to keep my blush to a minimum. I had a pretty tight rein on my reactions at the moment.

He walked me through the rest of the room talking to more old classmates, friends of the family, and neighbors. They were old, young, male, female, and I held my own. I wasn't quite as charming as Garrick. That wasn't humanly possible for me. Or most people, really. But I did okay. I watched people's expressions change as they talked to me. They went from wary or amused (probably due to my entrance) to smiling and accepting.

I took a deep breath, and felt proud.

Garrick brushed a kiss against my cheek, and said, "You're doing wonderfully. See? Nothing to worry about."

I smiled, but there was a sour taste on my tongue. It was a good thing . . . that I could force myself to fit here in his life. I just wished I hadn't had to be someone else to do it.

Almost as if she could sense my vulnerability, his mother made her reappearance then. She kissed Garrick's cheek, and surveyed his outfit. "Better. Much better."

She glanced briefly at my dress, but didn't say anything.

"Everything going okay? I saw you talking to Mrs. Everheart. Is she well?"

"When is she not well?" Garrick asked. "How old is she now, a century?"

Ah. I nodded, remembering who they were talking about now.

His mom shrugged. "Who knows? I wouldn't be surprised if she outlasted me just to spite all those grabby children of hers, *dying* for her inheritance."

I took a deep breath, and tried not to let it show how disgusting I found this whole thing. That old woman, Margaret was her name, had been *so sweet*. She reminded me of Cade's grandma, and the time he'd introduced us during college. She was kind, but you could definitely tell she was a firecracker underneath. That her own children would just see her as dollar signs was terrible. And that Garrick's mum and even Garrick didn't seem appalled by it . . . that was even worse.

Mrs. Taylor turned her eyes on me then, and said coolly, "So, Bliss, tell me about yourself?"

Not such a difficult question. But did I answer genuinely? Or did I tell her what she wanted to hear?

7

Garrick

BLISS HESITATED, THEN opened her mouth to speak. But she was interrupted by a bellowing voice calling my name.

"Garrick! Son!"

We both turned to look. My father called my name a second time. He waved me over and said, "Come here for a second."

I sighed.

"Just go," Mum said. "You know he won't let it go until you do."

"He's just going to drag me into some conversation about business. I don't want to subject myself to that, and I certainly don't want to subject Bliss to that."

"So leave her with me."

I tried not to look too alarmed by that. "Oh no, Mum.

That's okay. Bliss and I would rather stay together, since it *is* our engagement party."

"Nonsense. I'm sure Bliss could use a break from you anyway. If you're anything like your father, you're nauseatingly cheerful." That might be one of the nicer things I'd ever heard her say about him. "Besides, if you're only giving me a week with my future daughter-in-law, I'm going to need all the time I can get with her."

She spoke like a trainer trying to break in a horse, or an interrogator trying to break a witness. And from the look on Bliss's face, you'd think she was going to be waterboarded instead of subjected to conversation with my mother.

I stared into Bliss's wide eyes. I didn't want to leave her alone with my mother, but she *had* been holding her own since we came downstairs. And Mum had on her business smile, and I knew I wasn't going to win this one. Truthfully, there was no arguing with either of my parents. If my dad wanted me to go talk to him, I would have to. And if Mum wanted Bliss to stay with her, she'd get her way. That's why I hadn't bothered with telling them when I decided to leave London. God knows we'd spent enough time arguing about a thousand other things. Like a pendulum swing, the more I grew up, the farther I swung from my parents' beliefs and habits in every respect. So I'd waited to tell them I was leaving until I was already in the States and called from a pay phone.

My last year before uni, life just started moving so fast. Things were unraveling quicker than I could take hold of them, and it felt like trying to stop a boulder from rolling down a hill. My life was falling into these predetermined paths, and it didn't even really feel like I was living as much as reacting. I hated it, but I didn't know how to stop it, other than to leave. Clean slate.

My father called my name again, and I sighed. "Fine. But I'm not spending all night talking to clients or business prospects or whoever he's playing tonight.

"I'll be quick," I promised Bliss. Her expression was blank, and I couldn't tell now how she was feeling, but her frequently flushed skin looked a wee bit pale. I kissed her forehead, and then did the same to my mother.

"Be nice," I murmured.

Mum gave a single, solitary chuckle. That was either a very good or a very bad sign.

Two minutes. I'll be back in two minutes.

I gave Bliss one more parting kiss, and then feeling like the worst fiancé ever, I left her to fend off her shark while I faced mine.

Already eager for the conversation to be over, I stepped up to my father's group and said, "Yes, Dad?"

"Oh, good. Garrick, you remember Mr. Woods. You did that summer internship at his firm."

Advertising, I think? Honestly, I couldn't remember. Dad pushed me into so many internships, they all ran together.

"Of course, Mr. Woods. It's nice to see you again."

Mr. Woods was old, in his sixties or seventies maybe. He wore large glasses and his hair was a pale white. His smile made all the wrinkles around his mouth more pronounced, and his skin was worn and wrinkled like old leather as I shook his hand.

"And you as well. That's a lovely fiancée you have there."

I smiled. "Thank you. I love her very much, and she keeps my life interesting."

He barked a laugh, his wrinkles almost disappearing for a second as he did.

"You're just as spirited as I remember you. Your father has been filling me in on your life in the States. Quite impressive."

I resisted the urge to roll my eyes. My father had no doubt embellished to the point that I'd probably become the youngest tenured professor at Harvard or some other nonsense.

I shrugged. "I wouldn't say it was all that impressive."

"Not easily satisfied. I like that. You'll be outdoing your father in no time, I'm sure."

Dad laughed and hooked an arm around my neck like we were wrestling, "Not without a fight he won't."

It was all so staged, so forced. And I couldn't tell if everyone else felt it, or if they were so accustomed to it that they didn't even notice it anymore.

The men and women gathered around us laughed, and I followed out of habit.

Eight years.

It had been over eight years since I'd moved away, and in less than an hour, I was already getting pulled back into the lifestyle I hated. Fancy parties, nice things, expensive clothes, all covered by a layer of fake so thick that it choked out every real emotion.

It *had* to have been two minutes by now. And even that felt like two minutes too many.

"It was so nice seeing you again, Mr. Woods, but I should get back to my fiancée." I nodded at the rest of the people in the group and said, "Ladies. Gentlemen."

"Just one second before you run off, Garrick."

I stopped short, and tried not to look aggravated.

"Yes, Mr. Woods?"

Gradually, the others around us began to break off until it was just my old boss and my father.

"I wanted to talk to you about a job opening—"

Jesus. Not even a decent night's sleep before it started.

"Oh, sir, I—"

"Now hear me out. I have a PR position open, the same division where you did your internship actually. And I've been through half a dozen men in the last three years for this position. They're all smart enough, but they're just missing that special quality that attracts people, that makes clients feel at ease. They're not like *you* or your father." I tried not to bristle at being compared to my father and the quality I despised most in him. "I remember you doing fantastic work in your internship. And by the sound of what your father has told me, you're quick to adapt and learn." He pulled out a business card from his pocket and held it out to me. "Just think about it. Give me a call, and we'll talk it all through. It doesn't hurt to just consider it."

I looked at the card, but didn't take it.

"That's very kind, Mr. Woods. But Bliss and I have no plans to move to London." I directed my last few words to my father, as firmly as I could without seeming angry.

For the first time, my dad cut in and said, "Maybe it's something you *should* think about, Garrick. It's a good job."

I'm sure it was a fine job. But it wasn't a coincidence that this interest was coming now with my father watching on. He was a puppeteer pulling strings, but I'd cut mine a long time ago.

Mr. Woods added, "If it makes a difference, I'm sure it would be a significant step-up in pay from teaching, and we'd cover your relocation."

If it were a significant step-up from teaching, it would be about three or four steps up from what I was doing now. It had been difficult segueing back into part-time work and small contracts from my comfortable job at the university. But we were making it.

I took the card just to end the ambush and said, "I'll think about it. But I really am happy where I'm at."

I could feel my father's stare, but I didn't meet his gaze.

I nodded at Mr. Woods. "It was nice seeing you again. Thank you for coming. Enjoy the party."

Then I turned, and stuffed the card into my pocket. I made it just a few feet before my father stopped me for our first private conversation of the night. In years, really.

"I know what you're thinking, Garrick, but you should give this job a fair shot."

"I have a job, Dad." Several, actually.

"But this is a job that could really *lead* somewhere. If you keep doing what you're doing, you'll be forty and working at a restaurant to make ends meet. These kinds of opportunities won't be around then."

"Thanks for the confidence, Dad."

"Don't give me that. You're an adult. You don't need me in the stands cheering you on and lying to you. You're about to have a wife, a new life. What you need is to grow up and get a *real* job. Something with real benefits."

Oh, the irony of him lecturing me on what was real.

"Thanks for the talk, Dad. But I need to go find Bliss and Mum."

I maneuvered around him and left before he could drag me back into the argument. I was halfway across the room before I really looked around.

Bliss wasn't where I'd left her. And neither was my mother.

8

Bliss

GOD, HIS MOM should have been a lawyer instead of working in finance. Just her stare was like a fishing hook, luring all my secrets out of me. And I was the poor fish, dangling on the line, a rusty piece of metal tearing me open. An hour alone with her on the stand, and I would be in the fetal position, reciting the traumas of my childhood, like that time Jimmy pantsed me at the top of the slide during recess in third grade.

"And have you two set a date yet?"

I almost asked her if she would prefer to choose for us.

"Well . . . we're not set on anything yet. But we were thinking maybe June. Or August."

"Of next year? Oh, that could definitely work."

"This year, actually . . . ma'am."

"This year? But that's only a couple months from now."

"I know, but we weren't thinking of anything big. Just a small ceremony for close friends and family."

"But you won't have even been engaged for a year at that point."

This was one thing I wouldn't submit to her on. There was no way in *hell* that I was waiting over a year to get married. Garrick and I had had enough waiting for a lifetime.

"Yes, but we've been together over a year."

"No, you—" His mother stopped, her brows furrowed and one finger in the air. "Wait, you've been together *over* a year?"

I nodded, and then immediately wished I hadn't. Her eyes narrowed, and she fixed me with a look that was more sledgehammer than fishhook.

"I was under the impression that the two of you met in Philadelphia. But Garrick would have been teaching in Texas a year ago."

I swallowed. God, please don't tell me that Garrick hadn't told them about how we'd met. After he told Graham and his big speech about not lying or being ashamed, I had just assumed that he'd told them, the basics anyway.

Based on the calculating look on his mother's face, I was going to say that was a big, fat no. "So the two of you met in Texas?"

I tried to say yes, but really I just made noises and nodded.

"How old are you, Bliss?"

I could have narcolepsy! That would get me out of

this question, right? I could just pretend to pass out. Or maybe I could really pass out?

My non-answer must have been enough to confirm things for her because she spun on her heel and started in Garrick's direction.

I darted around her and held my hands up.

"Mrs. Taylor, wait. We didn't do anything wrong. I promise."

"Oh, sweetheart." Her smile gave me chills. "I don't think you did anything *wrong*."

"You don't?" I was shocked into silence.

"No, dear. My *son* is the one who has done something wrong."

I flinched back like she'd slapped me. I had enough doubts about Garrick being with me in my head, all of which seemed to have compounded in the hours since we'd arrived. I didn't need her adding any more to that. I stood up taller, and in my plain clearance dress, I faced off against her immaculate, no doubt heinously expensive cocktail dress.

"With all due respect, Mrs. Taylor. You're wrong. Your son loves me. And I love him. We're both adults, as we were when we met. If you make a big deal out of this now, you'll only ruin this party and possibly the already unstable relationship you have with your son. He's twenty-six, almost twenty-seven years old. He has a career and a fiancée, and you're not going to win any battles by treating him like he's a kid again. He's an *adult*," I reiterated, though that was another word that had been said and thought so many times it was beginning to lose its meaning. "We both are. How we met doesn't matter."

Her red lips flattened into a line, and her gaze felt sharp enough to slice bread. She made this sound in her throat, not quite a laugh, more like a noise of surprise. "You have a head on your shoulders after all."

Hey there, backhanded compliment. We've been seeing a lot of each other.

She was the one missing vital organs . . . like a heart. She stared at me for a few moments longer, and then smoothly turned her back to where Garrick was standing.

"Two questions, Bliss."

Did I really just talk her down? Holy crap.

"Yes, ma'am."

She clicked her nails together and looked away from me as she asked, "Would you like to have lunch on Thursday?"

I was so shocked, I nearly choked on my saliva, which would have totally ruined the whole head-on-your-shoulders moment from a few seconds ago.

I forced myself not to say, "Um," and continued, "Yes. Lunch. I would like that."

"Fantastic. And the last thing. You want to get married soon?"

"Yes, ma'am, we do."

"Are you pregnant?"

I blanched and said firmly, "*No.* Absolutely not. I'm not . . . we're not . . ."

I stopped. Full stop. Screeching-tires-stopped. I resisted the urge to reach for my day planner. I didn't have it anyway. I'd left it back in Philly. But I have a vague recollection of jotting down a note to get my birth control prescription refilled.

How long ago had that been? I'd been finishing up that run of *Peter Pan* and we were doing the maximum number of shows a week because it was selling so well. Things had been so busy, and . . . damn it.

"I—"

I closed my gaping mouth and gave her a tight smile. I shook my head and said, "No. Nothing like that."

Shit. Why was my memory such a blur? This is what happened when you worked multiple jobs with no consistency, and you did the same shows day in and day out. It became *really* fucking hard to distinguish one day from another.

Mrs. Taylor said, "Okay then. I'll let you get back to my son."

I nodded, already a thousand miles away.

"And Bliss?"

I lifted my head and met her cool gaze again.

"No more breaking things, okay?"

"Right." I gave a pained laugh. "Of course."

She walked away, her heels clicking against the marble floor, and I should have felt relieved to see her go. I should have been glad when Graham and Rowland came over to check on me, but I wasn't either of those things.

Because if I was remembering correctly, I was *late*.

And I was going to be sick.

"DIDN'T REALIZE YOU were that pissed. You must be a real lightweight."

Rowland and Graham were waiting when I got out of the bathroom, and I didn't know whether I wanted to find Garrick or avoid him, whether I wanted to scream or cry or throw up some more.

"I just . . . I need to sit down for a bit."

"We'll go in the sitting room," Graham said.

Damn it. This place *would* have a fucking sitting room. My parents were proud of their newly remodeled bathroom, and this place was practically a palace.

And the room was even nicer in real life than in my imagination. It was much more chic than the *Pride and Prejudice*-era room I had pictured. And there were people milling around, standing near the floor-to-ceiling windows and luxurious curtains. I found an empty cream-colored chaise lounge and collapsed onto it, too distressed to even worry about getting it dirty.

I could be remembering wrong. I *hoped* I was remembering wrong. But the last time I could recall being on my period had been that final week in *Peter Pan*. It's why I forgot about the pill pack because we weren't exactly in danger of getting pregnant then. And that was . . . what? Six weeks ago? Maybe five? Either way, it was more than a month. But sometimes people were late without being pregnant. That happened . . . right?

I could *totally* be jumping to conclusions.

Or there could be something *growing* inside of me.

God, that sounded so sci-fi movie.

What did I know about being a mom? What did I know about *anything?* I was a total mess. I couldn't even do my own taxes, or survive an engagement party, or turn on a fucking light without breaking something. And I was supposed to grow and raise another human being?

My child would be so socially inept that it wouldn't even be able to walk upright or speak in complete sentences or be around other people.

I would give birth to a hermit child.

Breathe. Breathe.

Damn it. That reminded me too much of Lamaze, and I felt sick again.

What if it turned out like Hamlet the devil cat and it hated me?

Shit. *Shit.*

I really just wanted to shout that word at the top of my lungs, but *probably* not the time and place.

"Is she okay?"

I opened my eyes to see a tall blonde, whose legs put mine to shame. She wore a short, black sheath dress with kick-ass turquoise heels, and there was basically a model standing over me as I panted and tried not to lose the remaining contents of my stomach.

Thanks, world. I appreciate it so much.

"Now is not a good time, Kayleigh," Graham said.

"Did something happen? They didn't break up, did they?"

Why did she sound hopeful?

Rowland spoke before I could, "No, she's just not feeling well. We'll find you later, Kayleigh."

"Oh, okay. Well, feel better."

I hated when people said that. Like I could just magically make that happen. Or like I didn't already want that desperately. But gee, thanks for the recommendation.

When she was gone, I looked at Rowland. "Who was that?"

He looked at Graham, and maybe some of Mrs. Taylor's perceptiveness rubbed off on me because I just had a feeling. "Is she an ex?"

"Ehh . . . umm . . . uhhh . . ."

This day could stop getting worse at any time. *Any* time now. Really.

"Why would his parents invite an ex to this?"

"Well, Kayleigh is a friend of the family. But we're guessing that Eileen, Garrick's mum, was keen on causing some problems because . . . well, Kayleigh's not the only one."

"Seriously? How many?"

Rowland looked at Graham again, and I was on the verge of strangling him. If I was pregnant, I could just blame it on the hormones. Call it temporary insanity.

"How *many*, Rowland?"

He scratched at his head. "Well, it's not like I've *counted*."

"Guess."

"Man, did Eileen give you some of her super powers?"

"Rowland," I snapped.

"I don't know, ten."

"*Ten?*"

Garrick had *ten* ex-girlfriends here.

Garrick had ten ex-girlfriends *before he'd even gone to college*?

And that was just the ones who'd showed up here. No telling how many more there were.

Hey, Universe? Think you could take a break on the whole raining-down-shit-on-Bliss thing? I'd appreciate it.

I stood to go back to the bathroom when Garrick stepped into the room. "There you are. I was a little worried my mother had killed you and was hiding the body."

I didn't laugh.

"Are you okay?" he asked.

I started to nod when Graham answered, "She's feeling sick. And she might have just met Kayleigh. And Rowland has a big mouth."

"Jesus."

He reached a tentative hand out to touch my shoulder.

"On a scale of one to ten, how angry are you?"

I pressed a hand to my temple, where a dull throb was beginning to form, and said, "Tired."

Rowland said, "Oh, well that's good."

I heard a *thwack* that I guessed was Graham smacking him upside the head.

Garrick laced our fingers together, and kissed the back of my hand. "Come on. We can go ahead and go to bed for the night. It's a bit early, but we can blame the jet lag. No one will miss us."

Only the ten ex-girlfriends here to get him back. Yeah, I was totally good with going to bed early.

I said good-bye to Rowland and Graham, and wished Rowland luck at landing one of the exes. Then I let Garrick lead me out of the sitting room, and toward the staircase that wound up from the dining room.

His mother intercepted us just before we got to the stairs. "Where are you two going?"

"Bliss isn't feeling well. And we're both still adjusting to the schedule. We're going to retire early. I think we've seen the majority of the people you care about us seeing."

I didn't look her in the eye, scared she would be able to read my mind with her freaky Slytherin stare.

"Oh, that's too bad. I have the guest room all set up for her."

Garrick tightened his grip on our luggage, and maneuvered around his mother and onto the first couple steps.

"That's not going to happen, Mum. Her luggage is already upstairs, and we're not accustomed to sleeping apart." I blanched. If he said that to *my* parents, he would be staring down a shotgun. "We'll be in my room."

I let myself glance at his mother. She took a deep breath, and then her eyes met mine. Despite feeling miserable, I squared my shoulders and raised my eyebrows in a look that I hoped said, *I told you so.*

As long as it didn't say, *I totally lied to you and might actually be pregnant after all.*

I followed Garrick up the stairs, still trying to wrap my head around this evening. Should I tell him? What if I was just remembering wrong? I didn't want to freak him out over nothing.

I should just wait. I'd keep thinking back. Maybe I'd forgotten something or was remembering the days wrong. Or I could go buy a test.

Yes. That's what I should do . . . to be certain.

I was so eager to brush my teeth that I didn't even say anything to Garrick before I retreated into the adjoining bathroom. And maybe I would just check *one* more time to make sure I hadn't started in the last ten minutes.

Garrick knocked on the door a few minutes later, and who would have ever thought I'd be *willing* my period to start?

His voice was soft, tentative. "Are you okay, love?"

"Yeah. I'm okay. I'll be out in just a second."

I took a deep breath.

There was no reason to panic yet. I'd told Eileen that I was an adult, and it felt good to stand up to her. To say that and actually *mean* it. It was especially important that I act like one now. Because if I was . . . if we *were* pregnant, there was a lot more at stake than a visit to meet the parents and a stupid broken vase.

So tomorrow I would get a pregnancy test. People did that all the time. And it came back negative *all* the time.

Tonight I just needed to put it out of my mind and get some rest. I would only make myself sick again worrying about it.

The bathroom door squeaked as it opened, and Garrick turned from where he was changing clothes. He was just sliding a pair of pajama pants up over his hips, and if that wasn't the perfect way to clear my thoughts, I didn't know what was.

9

Garrick

BLISS STOOD FRAMED in the bathroom door, and I was at a loss for how to act. I had no idea how things had gone with my mum or afterward. All I knew was that she was quiet. Too quiet. And as much as I didn't want her to be feeling ill, I hoped that that's all it was about.

"How are you feeling?"

She crossed her arms over her stomach and said, "Okay. I think it was just . . . a long day. And it got to me. I'm fine now."

"And my mother?"

"Should be a Disney villain."

I exhaled a laugh. Even sick and stressed she was . . . remarkable.

"But that was okay, too?"

After a torturous moment, she nodded. "I think so. We came to an understanding." That sounded ominous. "She invited me to lunch the day after tomorrow."

My eyebrows shot up.

"That means it went more than okay. It went well."

A small smile blossomed across her face. What was that science theory? Every action has an equal and opposite reaction? Seeing her smile lightened me. She anchored my thoughts, recentered my focus, balanced my life. And I needed that . . . desperately. Being back here . . . it was strange. I was struggling to walk that line between being polite and friendly, and falling back into my old ways.

"Now about these exes . . ."

Speaking of old ways.

"Exes?"

"Oh yes. Rowland estimated there were about ten in attendance."

Goddamn it, Rowland.

I closed my eyes to resist the urge to go downstairs and mangle him.

"I'm sure he was exaggerating."

The arms crossed over her stomach raised to cross over her chest, and she looked so deliciously bossy. Couldn't we just skip this part and get on to what we'd planned earlier?

"Do you have that many exes here in London?"

I wracked my brain for a way that this conversation wouldn't be disastrous.

"I don't know that *exes* is the right word."

"So they weren't all relationships? What . . . just sex?"

I grimaced. Guess we were cutting to the chase then. I didn't so much like this bold side of her when it was directed at me.

"Bliss . . . I was a right prick when I lived here. You would have *hated* me. My parents were not so good at the parenting aspect of life. They gave me money and a long leash, and like a stupid teenage boy, I took advantage of it. Often. Things are so beyond different now that that feels like a different life. A different person. And it was, really. When I left London, it was a rude awakening to live life outside this bubble of money and influence and tradition. But it was good for me. I grew up. I found something I *really* love, which led to finding *someone* I really love. If there were girls from my past here tonight, I didn't notice them. They don't matter. Nothing about this place matters at all in comparison to you."

She chewed on her bottom lip for a moment, surveying me. There was just a hint of a tear shining in the corner of her eyes, then she closed her eyes and shook her head. "It's impossible to be mad at you. This is setting a dangerous precedent for our relationship."

That was a good sign.

I stepped forward and settled my hands on her hips. "I like that precedent."

Her hands came up to my chest. "I know where you get it from. Your charm. Your father joins you and James Bond as a smooth-talking Englishman. He was really nice about the vase thing."

I groaned. "He is a smooth talker, yes. But don't let

him fool you. He's not nearly as nice as he pretends to be."

She traced her fingers along my jaw and pulled my face down toward her. "What does that mean?"

I shook my head. "Nothing you need to worry about. We just have different priorities is all. Business and money and class always come first to him." I laced my fingers at the back of her neck and grazed her jaw with my thumbs. "I may have inherited some things from him, but not that. You will always come first. Our family will always be my primary concern."

Her eyes were wide and glassy, and I didn't know if that look was because of something I said, or just the long day getting to her again.

She said, "It's funny how children end up being so different from their parents."

"It's funny how we managed to grow into reasonable people despite our crazy parents."

She swallowed and laughed once. "Right. How *does* that happen?"

I pulled her into my arms, laying my cheek against her head. Her hair smelled sweet and calming, like lavender.

"Let's go out tomorrow. I'll show you around the city. I just need a break from this house."

"Sure. That sounds great. I need to run to the store anyway. I forgot a few things."

I kissed her forehead. "Like what? We might have whatever it is."

She pulled back. "Oh, it's nothing important. Just some little things."

She went to her suitcase on the floor and bent to gather her pajamas.

I stepped up behind her. "You sure you're not feeling sick anymore?"

"No, I'm fine," she called over her shoulder. "I just had a moment, that's all."

"Good." I swept an arm under her legs and pulled her up into my arms. "Because I'm pretty awake. But I've got an idea of how to tire myself out."

She dropped the clothes she'd picked up to clutch my shoulders, and her pretty little mouth formed a circle. That was all it took. No matter that there were hundreds of people downstairs, and we were in my parents' house. I wanted her as badly as I ever had.

I walked her toward the bed and she said, "Garrick! The people downstairs."

"Won't hear a thing unless you plan on screaming my name. In which case, it might be worth it."

She swatted my shoulder, and I deposited her on the bed.

"What if your mother comes upstairs?"

I knelt at the foot of the bed and slipped off her shoes.

"Then we'll have another awkward occurrence to add to our repertoire."

"That's not even remotely funny, Garrick."

I kissed the inside of her knee and said, "Do you see me laughing?"

She swallowed, and her eyes followed my hands as I reached for her. Her cotton dress was stretchy, and I slipped the straps down over her shoulders easily. It fell around her waist, revealing more skin to me. She wore a lacy blue bra that looked sweet and innocent, and damn if that kind of thing didn't always do me in.

"Do you have any idea how hot it is to think of having you here in my old room?" She shook her head, but her tongue darted out to wet her lips, and I think she knew exactly what I meant. "It reminds me of last year." How much it had fucked with my brain to think of her as a student, and how very little it did to deter my feelings for her. If anything, I wanted her more. "Every class I was so tempted to ask you to stay after everyone left. Even though your friends were outside and anyone could have walked in, all I wanted to do was touch you. Taste you."

Her eyes were large and dark, and her breath hitched. I kissed the side of her knee again and ran my hands up her thighs to the hem of her dress.

She asked, "Why didn't you?"

"Because that wouldn't have been fair of me. So I had to settle for my imagination."

Thank God I didn't have to do that anymore.

"And what did you imagine?"

I leaned over her and laid her back against the bed. Her arms stretched out across the mattress, and she looked up at me with wide, apprehensive eyes. It reminded me so much of the night we met, and all my blood rushed south so quickly that black spots dotted my vision.

I slipped my hands under her dress and said, "I imagined a lot of things. I thought about having you against the wall back behind the curtains." She closed her eyes and fisted the blankets in her hands. "I saw you in that skirt you wore the first day of school with your legs around my waist."

I hooked my fingers around her underwear and slid them down her gorgeous legs. "I wanted you in every seat in the audience." She made a low noise and tried to sit up, but I braced a hand on her stomach to hold her in place. "I wanted you in every seat so that you wouldn't be able to sit anywhere in that theatre without thinking about me."

"That was already true."

I smiled. "Good to know."

She laid both of her hands over mine on her stomach, and held my hand tighter against her for a second. She said, her voice small and quiet, "I love you so much."

I stood and leaned over her so that I could see her face. She blinked a few times, and I couldn't read her expression. It was sad and happy and confusing, and she had *never* had this kind of response in bed before.

I didn't know what was going on, but I could feel the panic rising under my skin, at the back of my throat, in the lining of my lungs.

"Are you sure you're okay?"

She shook her head until her expression cleared, and then smiled. "Yeah . . . just thinking about the future."

My heart jerked in my chest, and I tried to explain away the sadness and the fear I saw in her eyes. They didn't have to mean she was having doubts. They could mean a thousand other things. But for the life of me, I couldn't conjure one more possibility.

I dropped a kiss on her lips and said, "I did promise you forever. That's a lot of future."

She nodded, and then after a too long moment she smiled. "I'm sorry. But do you think we can . . . just go to sleep? I'm sorry. I know I said I was fine, but I'm feeling a little off after all."

I took a deep breath and tried not to read too much into this. She'd been sick. It didn't have to mean anything else. But damn it, now I couldn't think about anything else.

As calmly as I could I brushed her hair back and kissed her forehead. "Of course. Can I get you something? Water? Medicine?"

She swallowed and shook her head. "I think . . . I think I just need some sleep."

I nodded. "Of course."

I folded down the blankets, and she slid between the sheets, still only half covered by her dress. I took another deep breath that did absolutely nothing to relieve the pressure in my jeans or the pressure in my head.

I kissed her cheek one more time.

"I love you," I said, slowly, deliberately. I needed her to hear that through whatever noise might be happening in her head. "Get some sleep. I'm just going to go take a quick shower."

"I'm sorry," she called again as I walked away.

"No need to be sorry, love."

Unless she was saying sorry for something else, something she hadn't said.

"I'll make it up to you," she said.

"Also not necessary, though I do like the sound of that."

She pulled the blankets up to her neck, settling back on the pillow. I switched off the lights and said, "Good night, Bliss."

Then I ended our roller coaster of a day with an ice-cold shower and too many worries to count.

"WAIT, WAIT! JUST one more!"

"Bliss, there are children waiting."

And they probably hated us, but I was just so glad to see her smiling that I didn't care.

"Yeah, well, they all just jumped on the bandwagon. Most of them weren't alive when I read Harry Potter for the first time."

I turned to the Canadian family behind me and said, "I'm so sorry. This is the last one, I promise." Then I took one more picture of Bliss pretending to push the luggage cart through the wall at the Platform 9¾ monument at King's Cross Station.

A little boy stuck his tongue out at Bliss as we left. I pulled her away before she could follow suit.

"That kid better watch it. I'm totally a Slytherin."

I shook my head, smiling.

"Love, I'm going to need you to pull back on the crazy a bit."

"You're right. Realistically, I'm a Ravenclaw."

I laughed. Even when I didn't quite get her, I loved her. Probably because I *didn't* get her. She knew who she was, and she didn't ever compromise that. Not even for me.

I chuckled.

"What's so funny?"

"I'm just imagining you with kids someday. You'll probably end up fighting them to play with the toys."

I didn't notice that she'd stopped walking until I went to round the corner, and she wasn't beside me. I turned and she was still standing a few feet back.

"I was *joking*, love."

She crossed her arms over her middle and shrugged. "I know that."

"Then why do you look so freaked out?"

"I just didn't realize you thought about stuff like that."

Oh God. The last thing I needed on this already stressful trip was to scare her off with talk of kids, not when she seemed mostly back to normal today. I could be really thick sometimes.

I laid my arm across her shoulders and said, "Whatever thoughts are unspooling in your mind, stop them. I've still got a lot to show you, and I was only having a laugh."

"Right, where to next?"

"Well, we've seen the Globe."

I felt her relax beside me as we walked, and she said, "You mean the replica of the Globe."

"Close enough. We've done Big Ben, the Parliament, the Tower. What about the Eye?" I asked.

"Is that the giant Ferris wheel thing?" I nodded. "Yes, let's do that!"

Just spending the day with Bliss and introducing her to my old city was enough to erase some of the messiness of last night, to erase some of my worries. She really must have just needed sleep because this morning, she was as perfect as ever.

"Can we stop by a store first?" she asked. "A pharmacy? I just wanted to get something in case I start feeling sick again."

"Of course," I kissed her temple, and we headed for the tube that would take us to the other side of the city.

10

Bliss

WE STOPPED AT a small store that was just a little bigger than a convenience store. It had food and toiletries and a random assortment of items, but the pharmacy in back was my concern.

"Would you mind grabbing me a drink?" I asked. "I'm going to run to the bathroom, grab that medicine, and I'll meet you back up here."

I didn't wait for Garrick to agree before I turned to walk away. I headed for the pharmacy at a stroll, glancing behind me to see when he was no longer looking. When he turned, I picked up the pace and began scouring the shelves for pregnancy tests. It took me three tries to find the right aisle, and then all I could do was just stare at the display.

Why did there have to be so many?

There were brand names and off brands, digital and sticks and cups, one lines and two lines and plus signs and the signs of the apocalypse.

And oh God, why was this so terrifying?

Maybe I should just get one of each.

Then I looked at the price.

Eh . . . probably just one would do for now.

I grabbed the stick one with the plus sign, and bolted for the pharmacy counter at the back. An Indian guy in glasses was typing away at the computer.

"Excuse me?" He looked up. "Can I check out here?"

"No ma'am. Cashier is up front."

Fabulous.

I grabbed a couple other things. Ibuprofen and sunscreen and a box of tampons (wishful thinking). I gathered all the items in my arms, hiding the pregnancy test behind them all. Then I went to the front to meet Garrick.

He stood holding a bottle of Coke, smiling and perfect, and God, I wanted to tell him. But his comment about kids earlier had my head all twisted. I'd thought about telling him then, but then he'd been so insistent that it was a joke that I started to worry that he would freak out. I mean, why wouldn't he? We'd only been together a year. We were just about to get married. There were probably prison cells roomier than our apartment.

I waited until it was our turn to check out and then I turned to him and said, "Oh honey, I'm sorry. Would you mind switching that out for a water instead? Or maybe juice? I just think that would be better for my stomach."

As soon as he was gone, I dumped all of my things on the counter and thrust the pregnancy test at the cashier.

"Can you ring this up first?"

The girl on the register was blond, couldn't be much older than sixteen, and she *laughed* at me. Actually laughed at me.

"Look, I realize this is crazy. But please. Just do it quick."

She shrugged and said, "He's going to notice sooner or later."

I *so* did not need attitude right now.

She scanned the test, and I shoved it in my purse just as Garrick came around the corner. He set the water on the counter, and then scanned my things.

"I thought you were getting medicine?"

Excuse me, sassy checkout girl, could I borrow your register for a moment to smash against my face?

I picked up the bottle of ibuprofen and shook it.

"I've been having headaches, and I think that's what caused the nausea."

The girl snickered when I said *nausea*. It probably didn't bode well for my future as a mother that I *really* wanted to punch this teenager.

Garrick took the bag from her as I paid and carried it outside for me. On the sidewalk, he said, "You could have told me. I'm not that naive."

I choked on the sip of water I had just taken and said, "What?"

He held up the bag, and I could see the box of tampons through the semi-transparent plastic. "This? The painkillers? You could have just said you were having your monthly."

Only I could suffer the humiliation of discussing a nonexistent period with my boyfriend.

"Oh, I'm not. No, these are just . . ." I totally blanked. "It was on sale."

He raised an eyebrow. "So you decided to buy it *now*?"

I was going to look into a career as a mime. Because that appeared to be the *only* way I was going to stop saying stupid things.

I took the shopping bag back and stuffed it in my giant purse. "How close are we to this Eye thing?" I asked.

We turned a corner, and he pointed up ahead to a giant white Ferris wheel. "Very close."

Glad for the change in subject, I listened to him explain that the Eye had been built while he was in school, and that on New Year's they actually fired off fireworks from the Eye itself. He explained that we'd board one of the pods while the structure was still moving, albeit very slowly.

We had to wait in line for a little while, but since it was a weekday it wasn't too bad. With our fingers laced together, we stepped to the front of the line, the first people to board the next pod.

Another ten to fifteen people boarded with us, and we found a spot at the window that would give us a good vantage point as the wheel continued its slow rotation upward. Garrick said one revolution was about thirty minutes, so I held on to the bar and he wrapped his arms around my waist. He placed his cheek against mine, and together we watched the city become smaller and smaller as we were pulled up into the sky.

The Thames twisted along beside us, steeples and skyscrapers punctured the clear blue day, and little dots of people moved below us in the distance. Up here they looked remarkably small, and there were so many. Some were in line for the Eye, others hustled along the busy streets. I could imagine each one of them wrapped up in their thoughts, contemplating their dreams, falling in love, getting news that changed their entire world.

In life, it's so easy to get tunnel vision, to imagine this world is a movie set and your story—what you see through your eyes and think with your brain and feel with your heart—is the only thing that matters. But the world was so much bigger than that. Life was so much bigger than that. Sometimes, I couldn't understand how it could hold all of us, all of the hope and hurt of humanity.

It was just as remarkable to think about the fact that at this very second, a new life could be forming inside of me. I didn't understand how I could hold that, either, how I could have another person who would be entirely dependent on me. The camera of my life was very focused. There was Garrick, of course, but both of us were concentrated on our careers, on establishing ourselves. But if we had a baby that would change everything for both of us. Our lens would have to refocus, adjust. It couldn't just be about us anymore.

I could feel the warmth of Garrick's hand against my belly through my thin shirt, and thought . . . the responsibility wouldn't be *entirely* on me. Yes, Garrick was a guy, and yes, most of them were terrified of commitment and babies and all those kinds of things. But he was different. This was a man that would hold my bag of tampons without any complaint, a man that didn't get angry when I stopped him right before sex, and a man that loved me and cherished me despite all my oddities and issues.

He interrupted my thoughts to point out the window. "Over there, that's where we were this morning. That's the church we walked by. And that way is my parents' place. You can also see the primary school I attended there. Graham and I were in trouble almost every day. Our mums threatened to send us both to boarding school."

It was the worst transition in the history of the world, but I looked over my shoulder at him and blurted out, "I bought a pregnancy test."

"What?" He didn't say it like he was shocked or horrified. More like when someone just didn't quite hear what you said.

So I continued, "At the pharmacy. I was being weird and sending you off to get drinks because I was buying a pregnancy test, and I was scared to tell you."

That time I got a reaction.

His hands dropped from their spot on my stomach, and he moved to lean on the bar beside me. His eyes searched my face, and I thought the silence would kill me, tie my windpipe into a pretty little bow, and suffocate my brain.

"Say something."

He opened his mouth, but nothing came out for several long seconds until, "You're pregnant?"

Okay. Correction. Say something that actually gives me a clue as to how you're going to react.

"I don't know. I'm late. I think. It could be nothing. "

"Or it could be something."

Damn it, why couldn't I read his inflection?

"It could be. Because . . . well . . . I forgot to refill my prescription. For the Pill. Things got busy, and it slipped my mind. It's still so new to me, and I—"

"Why didn't you tell me?"

I was going to go crazy if he didn't say something more definitive soon. I sighed and looked out at the city. We'd just reached the peak of the wheel, and the pod gave a panorama view of the city. I gripped the bar that kept people back from the glass and said, "I was scared. The thought of having a kid is *scary*. I still feel like a kid myself sometimes. And we both work so much, our apartment is tiny, we live in this huge, sometimes dangerous city that we can barely afford already, and we've not really talked about having kids. When they do get mentioned it's this vague, far-off thing in the future, and I didn't know how you would feel. So I was going to wait until I knew for sure. Or until I could get home to look at my calendar."

"But?"

My breathing was too loud in my ears, almost deafening. "But I didn't want to be scared alone."

His hands cradled my face, and he touched his forehead to mine. My breath hitched. He said, "You don't ever have to be."

I let out a small sob and held tight to him. He lowered one hand to my waist, his thumb brushing over my belly.

"Do you think . . . Do you *feel* like you are?"

I shrugged my shoulders. "I can't tell. I'm exhausted, but that could just be jet lag. I'm emotional, but that could be because I'm a social cripple who breaks expensive vases as a first impression. And I did get sick yesterday, but only once, so that could have just been the fatigue and shock."

He nodded, this time slipping his hand beneath my shirt to touch my stomach.

"If I am . . ."

"Then everything will be okay. All of those things you said are true, but we'll be okay. You will be an extraordinary mother, and we'll do whatever it takes to take care of our child." He smiled and shook his head, "Our child. Wow. That's what's was bothering you yesterday?"

I nodded, and he exhaled in relief. That was a good thing, right?

"Does that mean you're okay with this?" My heart was skipping.

"It means I love you and want to marry you and call you the mother of my child. It doesn't matter to me what order it happens in."

I leaned my head down against his chest, and suddenly the weight of my body felt like too much. His hand slid around to my back, and he pulled me in until my stomach pressed against his. I let him support more of my weight and said, "We do have a tendency to do things out of order."

"The world has given us plenty of surprises, but each one has turned out better than the last. I have no doubt that this will be the same."

He lifted my head up and caught my lips in a kiss.

We spent the rest of the ride ignoring the skyline for each other, and by the time the pod let us off back on solid earth, a really small part of me was actually beginning to hope for that plus sign.

11

Garrick

"THANK YOU FOR squeezing me in today, Mr. Woods. I really appreciate your time." He stood from behind his massive black desk, and came around to meet me.

"Nonsense. Anything for the Taylors. I'm just glad you decided to reconsider. You'll call me after you've talked to your fiancée?"

"Yes sir. I'll talk to her tonight."

"Fantastic. I think this could be a really good match, Garrick."

"Thank you, sir. I'll give you a call tomorrow."

A knot sat heavy in my stomach as I entered the elevator, and rode down the thirty-seven floors back down to the lobby. It had started yesterday when I'd called to set up the interview, and now it felt like it took up my entire midsection. Maybe it had actually started on the Eye. Or when Bliss took that first test, which had been negative. I'd almost canceled the appointment, but the instructions on the pregnancy test box suggested taking multiple tests, so I'd gone out to get another one.

That one had been positive.

Bliss took two more this morning, both negative, and we eventually decided that we were just testing too early. She wasn't sure exactly how many days she was late, but she guessed just a few, and everything we saw on the Internet suggested testing after a week.

So we decided to wait.

That seemed to be a staple in our relationship.

But whether she was pregnant or not, that didn't change the facts.

She was about to be my wife. We didn't have the money for a child any more than we had the money for a big wedding or a honeymoon. Neither of us had health insurance.

I loved acting, but how was I any different from my father if I chose to do that over providing for my family?

When Bliss had met me out on that empty stage after that performance of *Pride and Prejudice* and I'd gotten down on one knee, everything had changed. She had to be my priority. My job was to take care of her, and if that meant taking a job in London that made more money, then I would do it. Sure it was a job in my father's world, a world I had never wanted to be a part of, but I knew taking this job would make me different from my father, regardless of whether we appeared the same on the outside.

London had an even better theatre scene than Philadelphia, so Bliss could continue working here, and I'd make enough that she wouldn't have to work another job, she could just audition. And I . . . I would see her on stage, and that would have to be enough. I'd discovered my talent for theatre because pretending came so naturally to me. It was my way of life growing up. But I'd fallen in love with theatre when I found that it was the only kind of pretending that could also tell a truth. It would hurt to leave that behind, that feeling that I was a part of something bigger, something greater.

I would just have to learn how to find that same feeling in the audience.

Besides . . . marrying Bliss, starting a family, *that* was my something bigger.

The company would cover our move and health insurance. Baby or not . . . this made sense. It was the right thing to do. The smart thing.

I kept replaying all my reasons as the tube rocked back and forth on the tracks on my way back to Kensington. Bliss was out at her lunch with Mum, but we should be getting home around the same time. I needed to have all my thoughts laid out when I told her.

I wasn't sure how she'd react to the idea of leaving the States. She'd seemed really excited about coming to London, but visiting and living here were two very different things. But besides a slow start, she'd really held her own here. It was an almost seamless transition, actually. Even better than I'd hoped.

It would be okay. This would make everything okay. And Bliss could stop worrying about the pregnancy because this job would take care of everything. And after a couple years in this job, I could probably find a comparable one back in the States if she wanted to go back.

I arrived back at my parents before Mum and Bliss, and surprisingly met my father on the way in the door.

"Oh Garrick, I'm glad I caught you. I swung by to pick up some things on my lunch. How did the interview go?"

Of course he would know. I hadn't told anyone, but he must have heard it from Mr. Woods.

"It went well. I'm going to talk to Bliss about it tonight."

He nodded, pulling his BlackBerry out of his pocket after it buzzed.

"Good." He started tapping away at a message, and with his head down said, "You're making the right decision, Garrick. The smart one."

The knot in my stomach soured as he literally took the words right out of my head.

I wasn't like my father. We were different. This was different.

He left with one more proclamation that this was the right thing, and I had the massive, empty house alone to fill up with thoughts.

I'd taken a turn of pacing and sitting and stressing in nearly every room in the house by the time Bliss arrived home. It was hours after I expected them, and I was in the dining room, drumming my fingers against the long table, when the front door opened, and I heard laughter.

"Did you see her face? I haven't laughed so hard in . . . well, decades probably."

"I thought she was going to murder me, right there in the shop."

"I thought I was going to lose a lung laughing. You don't know how much I can't stand that woman."

I crossed into the foyer, and Bliss and my mother were smiling like the oldest of friends.

"What have you two been up to all day?" I asked.

Mum waved a hand. "Just causing a bit of mischief. It comes quite naturally to your future wife."

Of that, I was very well aware.

"And where have you been all this time?"

"Oh, here and there. Don't worry. I took good care of her. And I was *nice*, as you put it. To her anyway."

Bliss laughed, and whatever I was missing, it must have been one hell of a story. And I wanted to hear it . . . later. Right now I had about a thousand things to get off my chest, and I had everything I wanted to say arranged in my mind. I needed to say it before it all came tumbling down like a house of cards.

"I'm glad you two had fun, but can I steal her away for a while?"

"By all means," Mum said. "Steal away."

I held Bliss's hand as we climbed the stairs up to my room. I shook my head, chuckling. "Unbelievable. How do you do it?"

Deadpan, Bliss said, "I knocked down five racks of clothing at some upscale boutique she took me to. Seriously, it was horrifying. The most expensive domino line in the history of the world."

I burst out laughing.

She said, "That's about how your mother reacted, too. She was civil before that, but then it was like some kind of flip had switched. We had a blast."

This was a good sign. A great sign. Maybe she would *want* to be in London.

"My mother is all work. Today was probably the most fun she's had in ages."

"It was good for me, too," she said. "Listen, I—"

"I need to talk to you about something," I said.

"Oh." She frowned. "Of course. Go ahead."

I sat her on the edge of the bed, and out of habit my eyes went to her midsection. I think I'd looked at her stomach more in two days than in the entirety of our relationship before now.

"I did something today. Something a little crazy."

"Okay," she said tentatively, her fists clenched on top of her knees.

I blew out a breath.

"I interviewed for a job."

"You *what*?"

"I know, *I know*." I paced the length of the carpet in front of her. "I know it's out of nowhere, but an old boss talked to me about it at the party the other night. I didn't think anything of it until yesterday, but it solves all of our problems. The money is great, and they'll pay for us to relocate. We'll have health insurance to cover the birth.

We'll be able to afford to live in a very safe part of the city with good schools. You can audition here, and you won't have to worry about working any other jobs."

"You interviewed for a job here in London without telling me?"

"I haven't accepted it."

"You sure as hell better not have accepted it."

I was mucking this up completely. I forced myself to stop pacing and kneel in front of her on the bed.

"I know this is a lot. I'm only asking you to think about it, to think of all the problems it could solve."

"What about all the problems it creates? I'm already booked for a show in the fall."

"You'd have to give that show up if you're pregnant anyway. You'd be showing by then."

She stood, and then it was she who started pacing.

"We don't even *know* if we're pregnant yet. You want to uproot our entire life on a possibility?"

I took hold of her elbows and said, "No. No, of course not. We can wait to answer until next week, until we know for sure. But even if you're not pregnant, Bliss, you might be someday. This job is a rare opportunity. Most people have to work their way up for years to get this kind of job."

"And what kind of job is it?"

"What do you mean?"

She gripped my shoulders like she wanted to shake me. "What will you be doing? You love theatre. You said it made you grow up. It led you to me. You're going to leave that for what? A job behind a desk?"

"I love *you*, more than I've ever loved acting."

She pulled her elbows out of my grasp and threw up her arms.

"What does that have to do with any of this?"

"Bliss, I'm doing this for you. For us."

"Well, stop."

I shook my head. "What?"

"You heard me. *Stop.* I didn't ask you to do any of this."

"You don't have to ask." I dragged a thumb across her jaw. "I just think it's time for a bit of realism. It would be stupid not to take this job."

"I'm hearing a lot of stupid things at the moment."

Okay. So she wasn't excited about the idea of living in London.

"Damn it, Bliss. We need this. I'm trying to grow up, to get a real job, and be an adult about all this."

"Being an adult doesn't mean you change everything about yourself. You were an adult already without this fancy job and the money."

"But now I can be an adult that can provide for you."

"You already provide all I need. You said we needed a dose of realism?"

"Yes. We do."

I could see that now.

"You said almost the same thing to me on the first night we met, on the night we kissed. We were talking about theatre, about Shakespeare."

"Bliss—"

"I never would have even stopped at that table if you

hadn't been reading those plays. We would have met for the first time as teacher and student, and nothing would have happened between us. We might not have fallen in love if you hadn't been the assistant director for *Phaedra*. You proposed to me on stage, Garrick. Our whole life is theatre. The love we have is *because* of theatre. I associate all of our greatest moments with a play. If we'd thought about what was safe or smart when we met, we wouldn't be together today. And you'll always be the man that encouraged me to follow through on my dreams, the man that taught me how to make the bold choices and go after what I wanted. You said you weren't like your father. He's supposed to be the one whose primary concern is money."

"The money is just a means to an end. You and the baby are my priority."

"If you really want to do something for me, you'll turn down this job."

"Bliss, just think about it."

"I am thinking about it. I'm thinking about how I fell in love with a man who told a classroom full of seniors that the hardest thing about this life isn't landing roles or having enough money. It's keeping up your spirit and remembering why we chose theatre in the first place. So take your own advice, Garrick. You could have had this life all those years ago, but you didn't want it. You wanted something different. Something better. And either you still want that other life, that life with me. Or you don't. But I would leave before I'd let you ruin your own dream."

The silence detonated in my ears. My heart was raging in my chest, and I felt like my ribs were going to crack if it beat any harder. I *couldn't* lose her. I wanted her more than I wanted anything else. She eclipsed every dream, every desire, every doubt.

"Bliss—"

"I mean it, Garrick. I appreciate what you're doing, and I get it. I love you for being willing to do this, but it's not worth it. Not if you stop being *you*."

She took my hand and pressed it to her stomach. "If we did have a child, and he came to you with something like this, would you tell him to take the money, to take the job that didn't mean anything? Why am I even asking, I know what you'd say. You'd tell him to do the thing he loved, the thing that made him feel more alive. Life's too short to waste time living it any other way."

She was right.

Damn it. She was right.

The knot in my stomach loosened, and I released a heavy breath.

"How is it that you know me even better than I know myself?"

"Because I love you."

My heart sprinted, and the force of each beat drew me closer to her. Every time she said those words . . . *every time* it felt like the first time. I wrapped my arms around her and pulled until I had her feet dangling off the floor. I kissed the corner of her jaw and returned the words.

"But if we're pregnant . . . there are so many things we'll have to overcome. It's going to be hard with our life-styles."

She threaded her fingers through my hair and said, "Your mother took me to see a friend of hers who's a doctor."

I met her gaze, and set her feet back on the floor. "You told my mother?"

She shrugged. "That woman has a way of prying out my secrets."

"And?"

"And I'm not pregnant."

I swallowed, my stomach twisting with a combination of emotions, too vast for me to really identify.

"You're not?"

She shook her head. "The doctor said she thinks it's probably just stress that's thrown off my cycle. Probably the combination of all the work and thinking about meeting your family."

My heartbeat was slow, but loud in my ears.

"So . . . so we don't have to worry about any of those things."

"Not now, no."

For the life of me, I couldn't tell if I was disappointed or relieved. Not about the baby. The job though . . . that felt like I was a hundred times lighter.

"You okay?" she asked.

I kissed her forehead, then the tip of her nose, followed by her lips. I absorbed the calm from her warm skin, breathed in the balance from her closeness. I said, "Yes. I'm more than okay."

She nodded. Her expression was just as hard to read, and I got the feeling that she was just as confused about how she felt as I was.

"Garrick? One more question."

"Anything."

Her smile widened, brilliant and beautiful. All her confusion disappeared.

"Marry me?"

Half a dozen responses flitted through my mind, from simple to snarky. But there was one thing that would always be true about me. I preferred action to words.

So, I pulled her close and answered her as thoroughly as I could.

Continue reading for a sneak peek
at Bliss's best friend Kelsey's story in

FINDING IT

Coming in October 2013
from William Morrow

1

EVERYONE DESERVES ONE grand adventure.

We all need that one time in life that we always get to point back to and say, "Then . . . *then* I was really living."

Adventures don't happen when you're worried about the future or tied down by the past. They only exist in the now. And they always, *always* come at the most unexpected time in the least likely of packages.

An adventure is an open window, and an adventurer is the person willing to crawl out on the ledge and leap.

I told my parents I was going to Europe to see the world and grow as a person. (Not that Dad listened beyond the second or third word, which is when I slipped in that I was also going to spend his money and piss him off as much as possible. He didn't notice.) I told my professors that I was going to collect experiences to make me a better actor. I told my friends I was going to party.

In reality, it was a little of all of those things. Mostly, I was here because I refused to believe that my best years were behind me now that I'd graduated from college. I wanted to experience something extraordinary. And if adventures only existed in the now, that was the only place I wanted to exist, too.

After nearly two weeks backpacking around Eastern Europe, I was becoming an expert at just that.

I trekked down the old cobblestone street, my stiletto heels sticking in the stone grooves. I kept a tight hold on the two Hungarian men that I'd met earlier in the evening, and followed our two other companions down the street. . Technically, I guess it had been last night when we met since we were now into early hours of the morning.

I couldn't keep their names straight, and I wasn't even that drunk yet.

I kept calling Tamás, István. Or was that András? Oh well. All three were hot with dark hair and eyes, and they knew four words in English as far as I could tell.

American. Beautiful. Drink. And *dance.*

As far as I was concerned, those were the only words they needed to know. At least I remembered Katalin's name. I'd met her a few days ago, and we'd hung out almost every night since. It was a mutually beneficial arrangement. She showed me around Budapest, and I charged most of our fun on Daddy's credit card. Not like he would notice or care. And if he did, he'd always said that if money didn't buy happiness, then people were spending it wrong. So if he got mad, I'd just say I was finding my joy.

"Kelsey," Katalin said, her accent thick and exotic. "Welcome to the ruin bars."

I paused in ruffling István's hair (or the one I called István, anyway). The five of us stood on an empty street filled with dilapidated buildings. I knew the whole don't-judge-a-book-by-its-cover thing, but this place was straight out of a zombie apocalypse. I wondered how to say *brains* in Hungarian.

The old Jewish quarter—that's where Katalin said we were going.

Oy vey.

It sure as hell didn't look to me like there were any bars around here. I looked at the sketchy neighborhood, and thought at least I'd gotten laid last night. If I was going to get chopped into tiny pieces, at least I went out with a bang. Literally.

I laughed, and almost recounted my thoughts to my companions, but I was pretty sure it would get lost in translation. Especially because I was starting to question even Katalin's grip on the English language, if this was what *bar* meant to her.

I pointed to a crumbling stone building and said, "Drink?" Then mimed the action just to be safe.

One of the guys said, "*Igen.* Drink." The word sounded like *ee-gan*, and I'd picked up just enough to know it meant yes.

I was practically fluent already.

I cautiously followed Katalin toward one of the derelict buildings. She stepped into a darkened doorway that gave me the heebiest of jeebies. The taller of my Hungarian hotties slipped an arm around my shoulder. I took a guess and said, "Tamás?" His teeth were pearly white when he smiled. I would take that as a yes. Tamás equaled tall. And drop-dead sexy. Noted.

One of his hands came up and brushed back the blond hair from my face. I tilted my head back to look at him, and excitement sparked in my belly. What did language matter when dark eyes locked on mine, strong hands pressed into my skin, and heat filled the space between us?

Not a whole hell of a lot.

We followed the rest of the group into the building, and I felt the low thrum of techno music vibrating the floor beneath my feet.

Interesting.

We traveled deeper into the building and came out into a large room. Walls had been knocked down, and no one had bothered to move the pieces of concrete. Christmas lights and lanterns lighted the building. Mismatched furniture was scattered around the space. There was even an old car that had been repurposed into a dining booth. It was easily the weirdest, most confusing place I'd ever been in.

"You like?" Katalin asked.

I pressed myself closer to Tamás and said, "I love."

Tamás led me to the bar, where drinks were amazingly cheap. Maybe I should stay in Eastern Europe forever. I pulled out a two-thousand-forint note. For less than the equivalent of ten U.S. dollars I bought all five of us shots.

Amazing.

The downside to Europe? For some reason that made no sense to me they gave lemon slices with tequila instead of lime. The bartenders always looked at me like I'd just ordered elephant sweat in a glass.

They just didn't understand the magical properties of my favorite drink. If my accent didn't give me away as American, my drink of choice always did.

Next, Tamás bought me a gin bitter lemon, a drink I'd been introduced to a few weeks ago. It almost made the absence of margaritas in this part of the world bearable. I downed it like it was lemonade on a blistering Texas day. His eyes went wide, and I licked my lips. István bought me another, and the acidity and sweetness rolled across my tongue.

Tamás gestured for me to down it again, so I did, to a round of applause.

God, I love when people love me.

I took hold of Tamás's and István's arms and pulled them away from the bar. There was a room that had one wall knocked out in lieu of a door, and it overflowed with dancing bodies.

That was where I wanted to be.

I tugged my boys in that direction, and Katalin and András followed close behind. We had to step over a pile of concrete if we wanted to get into the room. I took one look at my turquoise heels, and knew there was no way in hell I was managing that with my sex appeal intact. I turned to István and Tamás—sizing them up. István was the beefier of the two, so I put an arm around his neck. We didn't need to speak the same language for him to understand what I wanted. He swept an arm underneath my legs, and pulled me up to his chest. It was a good thing I wore skinny jeans instead of a skirt.

"*Köszönöm*," I said, even though he probably should have been thanking me, based on the way he was openly ogling my chest.

Ah, well. I didn't mind ogling. I was still pleasantly warm from the alcohol, and the music drowned out the world. And my shitty parents and uncertain future were thousands of miles away across an ocean. My problems might as well have been drowning at the bottom of said ocean for how much they mattered to me in that moment.

The only expectations here were ones that I had encouraged and was all too willing to follow through on. So maybe my new "friends" only wanted me for money and sex. It was better than not being wanted at all.

István's arms flexed around me, and I melted into him. My father liked to talk, or yell, rather, about how I didn't appreciate anything. But the male body was one thing I had no issue appreciating. István was all hard muscles and angles beneath my hands, and those girls were definitely a-wandering.

By the time he'd set my feet on the dance floor, my hands had found those delicious muscles that angled

down from his hips. I bit my lip and met his gaze from be-
neath lowered lashes. If his expression was any indication,
I had found Boardwalk and had the all-clear to proceed to
Go and collect my two hundred dollars.

Or forint. Whatever.

Tamás pressed his chest against my back, and I gave
myself up to the alcohol and the music and the sensation
of being stuck between two delicious specimens of man.

Time started to disappear between frenzied hands and
drips of sweat. There were more drinks and more dances.
Each song faded into the next. Colors danced behind my
closed eyes. And it was almost enough.

For a while, I got to be blank. A brand-new canvas. Un-
touched snow.

I checked my baggage at the door, and *just was*.

There was no room for unhappiness when squeezed
between two sets of washboard abs.

New life motto, right there.

I gave István a couple notes and sent him to get more
drinks. In the meantime, I turned to face Tamás. He'd
been pressed against my back for God knows how long,
and I'd forgotten how tall he was. I leaned back to meet
his gaze, and his hands smoothed down my back to my ass.

I smirked and said, "Someone is happy to have me all
to himself."

He pulled my hips into his and said, "Beautiful American."

Right. No point expending energy on cheeky banter

that he couldn't even understand. I had a pretty good idea how to better use my energy. I slipped my arms around his neck and tilted my head in the universal sign of *kiss me*.

Tamás didn't waste any time. Like really . . . no time. The dude went zero to sixty in seconds. His tongue was so far down my throat it was like being kissed by the love-child of a lizard and Gene Simmons.

We were both pretty drunk. Maybe he didn't realize that he was in danger of engaging my gag reflex with his Guinness-record-worthy tongue. I eased back and his tongue assault ended, only for his teeth to clamp down on my bottom lip.

I was all for a little biting, but he pulled my lip out until I had one half of a fish mouth. And he stood there, sucking on my bottom lip for so long that I actually started counting to see how long it would last.

When I got to fifteen (*fifteen!*) seconds, my eyes settled on a guy across the bar, watching my dilemma with a huge grin. Was *shit-eating grin* in the dictionary? If not, I should snap a picture for Merriam-Webster.

I braced myself and pulled my poor, abused lip from Tamás's teeth. My mouth felt like it had been stuck in a vacuum cleaner. While I pressed my fingers to my numb lip, Tamás started placing sloppy kisses from the corner of my lips across my cheek to my jaw.

His tongue slithered over my skin like a snail, and all the blissful, alcohol-induced haze that I'd worked so hard for disappeared.

I was painfully aware that I was standing in an

abandoned-building-turned-bar with a trail of drool across my cheek, and the guy across the room was now openly laughing at me.

And he was fucking gorgeous, which made it so much worse.

Sometimes . . . the *now* sucked.

If you've missed any of Cora Carmack's
Losing It series,
read on for a look at where it all began . . .

LOSING IT

1

I TOOK A deep breath.

You are awesome. I didn't quite believe it, so I thought it again.

Awesome. You are so awesome. If my mother heard my thoughts, she'd tell me that I needed to be humble, but humility had gotten me nowhere.

Bliss Edwards, you are a freaking catch.

So then how did I end up twenty-two years old and the only person I knew who had never had sex? Somewhere between *Saved by the Bell* and *Gossip Girl*, it became unheard of for a girl to graduate college with her V-card still in hand. And now I was standing in my room, regretting that I'd gathered the courage to admit it to my friend Kelsey. She reacted like I'd just told her I was hiding a tail underneath my A-line skirt. And I knew before her jaw even finished dropping that this was a terrible idea.

"*Seriously?* Is it because of Jesus? Are you, like, saving yourself for him?" Sex seemed simpler for Kelsey. She had the body of a Barbie and the sexually charged brain of a teenage boy.

"No, Kelsey," I said. "It would be a little difficult to save myself for someone who died over two thousand years ago."

Kelsey whipped off her shirt and threw it on the floor. I must have made a face because she looked at me and laughed.

"Relax, Princess Purity, I'm just changing shirts." She stepped into my closet and started flipping through my clothes.

"Why?"

"Because, Bliss, we're going out to get you laid." She said the word "laid" with a curl of her tongue that reminded me of those late-night commercials for those adult phone lines.

"Jesus, Kelsey."

She pulled out a shirt that was snug on me and would be downright scandalous on her curvy frame.

"What? You said it wasn't about him."

I resisted the urge to slam my palm into my forehead.

"It's not, I don't think . . . I mean, I go to church and all, well, sometimes. I just . . . I don't know. I've never been that interested."

She paused with her new shirt halfway over her head.

"Never interested? In guys? Are you gay?"

I once overheard my mother, who can't understand why I'm about to graduate college without a ring on my finger, ask my father the same question.

"No, Kelsey, I'm not gay, so keep putting your shirt on. No need to fall on your sexual sword for me."

"If you're not gay and it's not about Jesus, then it's just a matter of finding the right guy, or should I say . . . the right sexual sword."

I rolled my eyes. "Gee? Is that all? Find the right guy? Why didn't someone tell me sooner?"

She pulled her blond hair back into a high ponytail, which somehow drew even more attention to her chest. "I don't mean the right guy to marry, honey. I mean the right guy to get your blood pumping. To make you turn off your analytical, judgmental, hyperactive brain and think with your body instead."

"Bodies can't think."

"*See!*" she said. "Analytical. Judgmental."

"Fine! Fine. Which bar tonight?"

"Stumble Inn, of course."

I groaned. "Classy."

"What?" Kelsey looked at me like I was missing the answer to a really obvious question. "It's a good bar. More importantly, it's a bar that guys like. And since we *do* like guys, it's a bar *we* like."

It could be worse. She could be taking me to a club.

"Fine. Let's go." I stood and headed for the curtain that separated my bedroom from the rest of my loft apartment.

"Whoa! Whoa." She grabbed my elbow and pulled me so hard that I fell back on my bed. "You can't go like that."

I looked down at my outfit—flowery A-line skirt and simple tank that showed a decent amount of cleavage. I looked cute. I could totally pick up a guy in this . . . maybe.

"I don't see the problem," I said.

She rolled her eyes, and I felt like a child. I hated feeling like a child, and I pretty much always did when talk turned to sex.

Kelsey said, "Honey, right now you look like someone's adorable little sister. No guy wants to screw his little sister. And if he does, you don't want to be near him."

Yep, definitely felt like a child. "Point taken."

"Hmm . . . sounds like you're practicing turning off that overactive brain of yours. Good job. Now stand there and let me work my magic."

And by magic, she meant torture.

After vetoing three shirts that made me feel like a prostitute, some pants that were more like leggings, and a skirt so short it threatened to show the world my hoo-hoo in the event of a mild breeze, we settled on some tight low-rise denim capris and a lacy black tank that stood out in contrast to my pale white skin.

"Legs shaved?"

I nodded.

"Other . . . things . . . shaved?"

"As much as they are ever going to be, yes, now move on." That was where I drew the line of this conversation.

She grinned, but didn't argue. "Fine. Fine. Condoms?"

"In my purse."

"Brain?"

"Turned off. Or well . . . dialed down anyway."

"Excellent. I think we're ready."

I wasn't ready. Not at all.

There was a reason I hadn't had sex yet, and now I knew it. I was a control freak. It was why I had done so well in school my entire life. It made me a great stage manager—no one could run a theater rehearsal like I could. And when I did get up the nerve to act, I was always more prepared than any other actor in class. But sex . . . that was the opposite of control. There were emotions, and attraction, and that pesky other person that just *had* to be involved. Not my idea of fun.

"You're thinking too much," Kelsey said.

"Better than not thinking enough."

"Not tonight it's not," she said.

I turned up the volume of Kelsey's iPod as soon as we got in the car so that I could think in peace.

I could do this. It was just a problem that needed to be solved, an item that needed to be checked off my to-do list.

It was that simple.

Simple.

Keep it simple.

We pulled up outside the bar several minutes later, and the night felt anything but simple. My pants felt too tight, my shirt too low-cut, and my brain too clouded. I wanted to throw up.

I didn't want to be a virgin. That much I knew. I didn't want to feel like the immature prude who knew nothing about sex. I hated not knowing things. The trouble was . . . as much as I didn't want to be a virgin, I also didn't want to have sex.

The conundrum of all conundrums. Why couldn't this be one of those square-is-a-rectangle-but-rectangle-is-not-always-a-square kind of things?

Kelsey was standing outside my door, her high-heeled shoes snapping in time with her fingers as she roused me out of the car. I squared my shoulders, tossed my hair (halfheartedly), and followed Kelsey into the bar.

I made a beeline straight to the bar, wiggled myself onto a stool, and waved down the bartender.

He was a possibility. Blond hair, average build, nice face. Nothing special, but certainly not out of the question. He could be good for simple.

"What can I get for y'all, ladies?"

Southern accent. Definitely a homegrown kind of boy. Kelsey butted in, "We need two shots of tequila to start."

"Make it four," I croaked.

He whistled, and his eyes met mine. "That kinda night, huh?"

I wasn't ready to put into words what kind of night this was. So I just said, "I'm looking for some liquid courage."

"And I'd be glad to help." He winked at me, and he was barely out of earshot before Kelsey bounced in her seat, saying, "He's the one! He's the one!"

Her words made me feel like I was on a roller coaster, like the world had just dropped and all my organs were playing catch-up. I just needed more time to adjust. That's it. I grabbed Kelsey's shoulder and forced her to stay still. "Chill, Kels. You're like a freaking Chihuahua."

"What? He's a good choice. Cute. Nice. And I totally saw him glance at your cleavage . . . *twice*."

She wasn't wrong. But I still wasn't all that interested in sleeping with him, which I suppose didn't have to rule him out, but this sure would be a hell of a lot easier if I was actually *interested* in the guy. I said, "I'm not sure . . . there's just no spark." I could see an eye roll coming, so I tagged on a quick "Yet!"

When Bartender Boy returned with our drinks, Kelsey paid and I took my two shots before she even handed over her card. He stayed for a moment, smiling at me, before moving on to another customer. I stole one of Kelsey's remaining shots.

"You're lucky this is a big night for you, Bliss. Normally, nobody gets between me and my tequila."

I held my hand out and said, "Well, nobody will get between these legs unless I'm good and drunk, so hand me the last one."

Kelsey shook her head, but she was smiling. After a few seconds, she gave in, and with four shots of tequila in my system the prospect of sex seemed a little less scary.

Another bartender came by, this one a girl, and I ordered a Jack and Coke to sip on while I puzzled through this whole mess.

There was Bartender Boy, but he wouldn't get off until well after 2:00 A.M. I was a nervous wreck already, so if this dragged on till the wee hours of the morning, I'd be completely psychotic. I could just imagine it . . . strait-jacketed due to sex.

There was a guy standing next to me who seemed to move several inches closer with every drink I took, but he had to be at least forty. No thank you.

I gulped down more of my drink, thankful the bartender had gone heavy on the Jack, and scanned the bar.

"What about him?" Kelsey asked, pointing to a guy at a nearby table.

"Too preppy."

"Him?"

"Too hipster."

"Over there?"

"Ew. Too hairy."

The list continued until I was pretty sure this night was a bust. Kelsey suggested we hit another bar, which was the last thing I wanted to do. I told her I had to go to the bathroom, hoping someone would catch her eye while I was gone so that I could slip away with no drama. The bathroom was at the back, past the pool and darts area, behind a section with some small round tables.

That was when I noticed him.

Well, technically, I noticed the book first.

And I just couldn't keep my mouth closed. "If that's supposed to be a way to pick up girls, I would suggest moving to an area with a little more traffic."

He looked up from his reading, and suddenly I found it hard to swallow. He was easily the most attractive guy I'd seen tonight—blond hair falling into crystal blue eyes, just enough scruff on his jaw to give him a masculine look without making him too hairy, and a face that could have made angels sing. It wasn't making me sing. It was making me gawk. Why did I stop? Why did I always have to make an idiot of myself?

"Excuse me?"

My mind was still processing his perfect hair and bright blue eyes, so it took me a second to say, "Shakespeare. No one reads Shakespeare in a bar unless it's a ploy to pick up girls. All I'm saying is, you might have better luck up front."

He didn't say anything for a long beat, but then his mouth split in a grin revealing, what do you know, perfect teeth!

"It's not a ploy, but if it were, it seems to me that I'm having great luck right here."

An accent. *He has a British accent.* Dear God, I'm dying.

Breathe. I needed to breathe.

Don't lose it, Bliss.

He put his book down, but not before marking his place. My God, he was really reading Shakespeare in a bar.

"You're not trying to pick up a girl?"

"I wasn't."

My analytical brain did not miss his use of the past tense. As in . . . he hadn't been trying to seduce anyone before, but perhaps he was now.

I took another look at him. He was grinning now—

white teeth, jaw stubble that made him look downright delectable. Yep, I was definitely seducible. And that thought alone was enough to send me into shock.

"What's your name, love?"

Love? *Love!* Still dying here.

"Bliss."

"Is that a line?"

I blushed crimson. "No, it's my name."

"Lovely name for a lovely girl." The timbre of his voice went into that low register that made my insides curl in on themselves—it was like my uterus was tapping out a happy dance on the rest of my organs. God, I was dying the longest, most torturous, most arousing death in the history of the world. Was this what it always felt like to be turned on? No wonder sex made people do crazy things.

"Well, Bliss, I'm new in town, and I've already locked myself out of my apartment. I'm waiting on a locksmith actually, and I figured I'd put this spare time to good use."

"By brushing up on your Shakespeare?"

"Trying to anyway. Honestly, I've never liked the bloke all that much, but let's keep that a secret between us, yeah?"

I'm pretty sure my cheeks were still stained red, if the heat coming off of them was any indication. In fact, my whole body felt like it was on fire. I'm not sure whether it was mortification or his accent that had me about to spontaneously combust in front of him.

"You look disappointed, Bliss. Are you a Shakespeare fan?"

I nodded, because my throat might have been closing up.

He wrinkled his nose in response, and my hands itched to follow the line of his nose down to his lips.

I was going crazy. Actually, certifiably insane.

"Don't tell me you're a *Romeo and Juliet* fan?"

Now this. *This* was something I could discuss.

"*Othello* actually. That's my favorite."

"Ah. Fair Desdemona. Loyal and pure."

My heart stuttered at the word "pure."

"I, um . . ." I struggled to piece together my thoughts. "I like the juxtaposition of reason and passion."

"I'm a fan of passion myself." His eyes dipped down then and ran the length of my form. My spine tingled until it felt like it might burst out of my skin.

"You haven't asked me my name," he said.

I cleared my throat. This couldn't be attractive. I was about as sociable as a caveman. I asked, "What's your name?"

He tilted his head, and his hair almost covered his eyes.

"Join me, and I'll tell you."

I didn't think about anything other than the fact that my legs were like Jell-O and sitting down would prevent me from doing something embarrassing, like passing out from the influx of hormones that were quite clearly having a free-for-all in my brain. I sank into the chair, but instead of feeling relieved, the tension ratcheted up another notch.

He spoke, and my eyes snagged on his lips. "My name is Garrick."

Who knew names could be hot too?

"It's nice to meet you, Garrick."

He leaned forward on his elbows, and I noticed his broad shoulders and the way his muscles moved beneath the fabric of his shirt. Then our eyes connected, and the bar around us went from dim to dark, while I was ensnared by those baby blues.

"I'm going to buy you a drink." It wasn't meant to be a question. In fact, when he looked at me, there was nothing questioning in him at all, only confidence. "Then we can chat some more about reason and . . . passion."

FAKING IT

PART III

1

Cade

YOU WOULD THINK I'd be used to it by now. That it wouldn't feel like a rusty eggbeater to the heart every time I saw them together.

You would think I would stop subjecting myself to the torture of seeing the girl I loved with another guy.

You would be wrong on all counts.

A nor'easter had just blown through, so the Philadelphia air was crisp. Day-old snow still crunched beneath my boots. The sound seemed unusually loud, like I walked toward the gallows instead of coffee with friends.

Friends.

I gave one of those funny-it's-not-actually-funny laughs, and my breath came out like smoke. I could see them standing on the corner up ahead. Bliss's arms were wound around Garrick's neck, and the two of them stood wrapped together on the sidewalk. Bundled in coats and scarves, they could have been a magazine ad or one of those perfect pictures that come in the frame when you buy it.

I hated those pictures.

I tried not to be jealous. I was getting over it.

I was.

I wanted Bliss to be happy, and as she slipped her hands in Garrick's coat pockets and their breath fogged between them, she definitely looked happy. But that was part of the problem. Even if I managed to let go of my feelings for Bliss completely, it was their happiness that inspired my jealousy.

Because I was fucking miserable. I tried to keep myself busy, made some friends, and settled into life all right here, but it just wasn't the same.

Starting over sucked.

On a scale of one to ghetto, my apartment was a solid eight. Things were still awkward with my best friend. I had student loans piling so high I might asphyxiate beneath them at any time. I thought by pursuing my master's degree, I would get at least one part of my life right . . . WRONG.

I was the youngest one in the program, and everyone else had years of working in the real world under his or her belt. They all had their lives together, and my life was about as clean and well kept as the community bathrooms had been in my freshman dorm. I'd been here nearly three months, and the only acting I'd done had been a cameo appearance as a homeless person in a Good Samaritan commercial.

Yeah, I was living the good life.

I knew the minute Bliss caught sight of me because she pulled her hands out of Garrick's pockets, and placed them safely at her sides. She stepped out of his arms and called, "Cade!"

I smiled. Maybe I was doing *some* acting after all.

I met them on the sidewalk, and Bliss gave me a hug. Short. Obligatory. Garrick shook my hand. As much as it irked me, I still really liked the guy. He'd never tried to keep Bliss from seeing me, and he'd apparently given me a pretty stellar reference when I applied to Temple. He didn't go around marking his territory or telling me to back off. He shook my hand and smiled, and sounded genuine when he said, "It's good to see you, Cade."

"Good to see you guys, too."

There was a moment of awkward silence, and then Bliss gave an exaggerated shiver. "I don't know about you guys, but I'm freezing. Let's head inside."

Together we filed through the door. Mugshots was a coffee place during the day and served alcohol at night. I'd not been there yet, as it was kind of a long trek from my apartment up by the Temple campus and because I didn't drink coffee, but I'd heard good things. Bliss loved coffee, and I still loved making Bliss happy, so I agreed to meet there when she called. I thought of asking if they'd serve me alcohol now, even though it was morning. Instead I settled on a smoothie and found us a table big enough that we'd have plenty of personal space.

Bliss sat first while Garrick waited for their drinks. Her cheeks were pink from the cold, but the winter weather agreed with her. The blue scarf knotted around her neck brought out her eyes, and her curls were scattered across her shoulders, windswept and wonderful.

Damn it. I had to stop doing this.

She pulled off her gloves, and rubbed her hands together. "How are you?" she asked.

I balled my fists under the table and lied. "I'm great. Classes are good. I'm loving Temple. And the city is great. I'm great."

"You are?" I could tell by the look on her face that she knew I was lying. She was my best friend, which made her pretty hard to fool. She'd always been good at reading me . . . except for when it came to how I felt about her. She could pick up on just about all my other fears and insecurities, but never that. Sometimes I wondered if it was wishful thinking. Maybe she never picked up on my feelings because she hadn't wanted to.

"I am," I assured her. She still didn't believe me, but she knew me well enough to know that I needed to hold on to my lie. I couldn't vent to her about my problems, not right now. We didn't have that kind of relationship anymore.

Garrick sat down. He'd brought all three of our drinks. I didn't even hear them call out my order.

"Thanks," I said.

"No problem. What are we talking about?"

Here we go again.

I took a long slurp of my smoothie so that I didn't have to answer immediately.

Bliss said, "Cade just finished telling me all about his classes. He's kicking higher education's ass." At least some things hadn't changed. She still knew me well enough to know when I needed an out.

Garrick nudged Bliss's drink toward her and smiled when she took a long, grateful drink. He turned to me and said, "That's good to hear, Cade. I'm glad it's going well. I'm still on good terms with the professors at Temple, so if you ever need anything, you know you just have to ask."

God, why couldn't he have been an asshole? If he were, one good punch would have gone a long way to easing the tightness in my chest. And it would be much cheaper than punching out a wall in my apartment.

I said, "Thanks. I'll keep that in mind."

We chattered about unimportant things. Bliss talked about their production of *Pride and Prejudice*, and I realized that Garrick really had been good for her. I never would have guessed that out of all of us, she'd be the one doing theatre professionally so quickly after we graduated. It's not that she wasn't talented, but she was never confident. I thought she would have gone the safer route and been a stage manager. I liked to think I could have brought that out of her, too, but I wasn't so sure.

She talked about their apartment on the edge of the Gayborhood. So far, I'd managed to wriggle out of all her invitations to visit, but sooner or later I was going to run out of excuses and would have to see the place they lived. Together.

Apparently their neighborhood was a pretty big party area. They lived right across from a really popular bar. Garrick said, "Bliss is such a light sleeper that it has become a regular event to wake up and listen to the drama that inevitably occurs outside our window at closing time."

She was a light sleeper? I hated that he knew that and I didn't. I hated feeling this way. They started relaying a story of one of those nighttime events, but they were barely looking at me. They stared at each other, laughing, reliving the memory. I was a spectator to their perfect harmony, and it was a show I was tired of watching.

I made a promise to myself then that I wouldn't do this again. Not until I had figured all my shit out. This had to be the last time. I smiled and nodded through the rest of the story, and was relieved when Bliss's phone rang.

She looked at the screen, and didn't even explain before she accepted the call and pressed the phone to her ear. "Kelsey? Oh my God! I haven't heard from you in weeks!"

Kelsey had done exactly what she said she would. At the end of the summer, everyone was moving to new cities or new universities, and Kelsey went overseas for the trip of a lifetime. Every time I looked at Facebook, she had added a new country to her list.

Bliss held up a finger and mouthed, "Be right back." She stood and said into the phone, "Kelsey, hold on one sec. I can barely hear you. I'm going to go outside."

I watched her go, remembering when her face used to light up like that talking to me. It was depressing the way life branched off in different directions. Trees only grew up and out. There was no going back to the roots, to the way things had been. I'd spent four years with my college friends, and they felt like family. But now we were scattered across the country and would probably never be all together again.

Garrick said, "Cade, there's something I'd like to talk to you about while Bliss is gone."

This was going to suck. I could tell. Last time we'd had a chat alone, he'd told me that I had to get over Bliss, that I couldn't live my life based on my feelings for her. Damn it if he wasn't still right.

"I'm all ears," I said.

"I don't really know the best way to say—"

"Just say it." That was the worst part of all of this. I'd gotten my heart broken by my best friend, and now everyone tiptoed around me like I was on the verge of meltdown, like a girl with PMS. Apparently having emotions equated to having a vagina.

Garrick took a deep breath. He looked unsure, but in the moments before he spoke, a smile pulled at his face, like he just couldn't help himself.

"I'm proposing to Bliss," he said.

The world went silent, and I heard the *tick-tick* of the clock on the wall beside us. It sounded like the ticking of a bomb, which was ironic, considering all the pieces of me that I had been holding together by sheer force of will had just been blown to bits.

I schooled my features as best as I could even though I felt like I might suffocate at any moment. I took a beat, which is just a fancy acting word for a pause, but it felt easier if I approached this like a scene, like fiction. Beats are reserved for those moments when something in the scene or your character shifts. They are moments of change.

Man, was this one hell of a beat.

"Cade—"

Before Garrick could say something nice or consoling, I pushed my character, pushed myself back into action. I smiled and made a face that I hoped look congratulatory.

"That's great, man! She couldn't have found a better guy."

It really was just like acting, bad acting anyway. Like when the words didn't feel natural in my mouth and my mind stayed separate from what I was saying no matter how hard I tried to stay in character. My thoughts raced ahead, trying to judge whether or not my audience was buying my performance, whether Garrick was buying it.

"So, you're okay with this?"

It was imperative that I didn't allow myself to pause before I answered, "Of course! Bliss is my best friend, and I've never seen her so happy, which means I couldn't be happier for her. The past is the past."

He reached across the table and patted me on the shoulder, like I was his son or little brother or his dog.

"You're a good man, Cade."

That was me . . . the perpetual good guy, which meant

I perpetually came in second. My smoothie tasted bitter on my tongue.

"You had auditions last week, right?" Garrick asked. "How did they turn out?"

Oh please no. I just had to hear about his proposal plans. If I had to follow that up by relaying my complete and utter failure as a grad student, I'd impale myself on a stirring straw.

Luckily I was saved by Bliss's return. She was tucking her phone back into her pocket, and had a wide smile on her face. She stood behind Garrick's chair and placed a hand on his shoulder. I was struck suddenly by the thought that she was going to say yes.

Somewhere deep in my gut, I could feel the certainty of it. And it killed me.

Beat.

Beat.

Beat.

I should say something, anything, but I was stalled. Because this wasn't fiction. This wasn't a play, and we weren't characters. This was my life, and change had a way of creeping up and stabbing me in the back.

Oblivious, Bliss turned to Garrick and said, "We have to go, babe. We have call across town in like thirty minutes." She turned to me, "I'm sorry, Cade. I meant for us to have more time to chat, but Kelsey's been MIA for weeks. I couldn't not answer, and we've got a matinee for a group of students today. I swear I'll make it up to you. Are you going to be able to make it to our Orphan Thanksgiving tomorrow?"

I'd been dodging that invitation for weeks. I was fairly certain that it had been the entire purpose of this coffee meeting. I'd been on the verge of giving in, but now I couldn't. I didn't know when Garrick planned to propose, but I couldn't be around when it happened or after it happened. I needed a break from them, from Bliss, from being a secondary character in their story.

"Actually, I forgot to tell you. I'm going to go home for Thanksgiving after all." I hated lying to her, but I just couldn't do it anymore. "Grams hasn't been feeling well, so I thought it was a good idea to go."

Her face pulled into an expression of concern, and her hand reached out toward my arm. I pretended like I didn't see it and stepped away to throw my empty smoothie cup in the trash. "Is she okay?" Bliss asked.

"Oh yeah, I think so. Just a bug probably, but at her age, you never know."

I just used my seventy-year-old grandma, the woman who'd raised me, as an excuse. Talk about a douche move.

"Oh, well, tell her I said hi and that I hope she feels better. And you have a safe flight." Bliss leaned in to hug me, and I didn't move away. In fact, I hugged her back. Because I didn't plan on seeing her again for a while, not until I could say (without lying) that I was over her. And based on the way my whole body seemed to sing at her touch, it might take a while.

The two of them packed up to leave, and I sat back

down, saying I was going to stay and work on homework for a while. I pulled out a play to read, but in reality, I just wasn't ready for the walk home. I couldn't spend any more alone time locked in my thoughts. The coffee shop was just busy enough that my mind was filled with the buzzing of other people's lives and conversations. Bliss waved through the glass as they left, and I waved back, wondering if she could feel the finality of this good-bye.

2

Max

MACE'S HAND SLID into my back pocket at the same time the phone in my front pocket buzzed. I let him have the three seconds it took for me to grab my phone, then I elbowed him, and he removed his hand.

I'd had to elbow him three times on the way to the coffee shop. He was like that cartoon fish with memory problems.

I looked at the screen, and it showed a picture of my mom that I'd snapped while she wasn't looking. She had been chopping vegetables and looked like a knife-wielding maniac, which she pretty much was all the time, minus the knife.

I jogged the last few steps to Mugshots and slipped inside before answering.

"Hello, Mom."

There was Christmas music on in the background. We hadn't even got Thanksgiving over with, and she was playing Christmas music.

Maniac.

"Hi, sweetie!" She stretched out the end of *sweetie* so long I thought she was a robot who had just malfunctioned. Then finally she continued, "What are you up to?"

"Nothing, Mom. I just popped into Mugshots for a coffee. You remember, it was that place I took you when you and Dad helped me move here."

"I do remember! It was a cute place, pity they serve alcohol."

And there was my mom in a nutshell.

Mace chose that moment (an unfortunately silent moment) to say, "Max, babe, you want your usual?"

I waved him off, and stepped a few feet away.

Mom must have had me on speakerphone because my dad cut in, "And who is that, Mackenzie?"

Mackenzie.

I shuddered. I hated my parents' absolute refusal to call me Max. And if they didn't approve of Max for their baby girl, they sure wouldn't like that I was dating a guy named Mace.

My dad would have an aneurysm.

"Just a guy," I said.

Mace nudged me and rubbed his thumb and fingers together. That's right. He'd been fired from his job. I handed him my purse to pay.

"Is this a guy you're dating?" Mom asked.

I sighed. There wasn't any harm in giving her this, as long as I fudged some of the details. Or you know, all of them.

"Yes, Mom. We've been dating for a few weeks." Try three months, but whatever.

"Is that so? How come we don't know anything about this guy then?" Dad, again.

"Because it's still new. But he's a really nice guy, smart." I don't think Mace actually finished high school, but he was gorgeous and a killer drum player. I wasn't cut out for the type of guy my mother wanted for me. My brain would melt from boredom in a week. That was if I didn't send him running before that.

"Where did you meet?" Mom asked.

Oh, you know, he hit on me at the go-go bar where I dance, that extra job that you have no idea I work.

Instead, I said, "The library."

Mace at the library. That was laughable. The tattoo curving across his collarbone would have been spelled *villian* instead of *villain* if I hadn't been there to stop him.

"Really?" Mom sounded skeptical. I didn't blame her. Meeting nice guys at the library wasn't really my thing. Every meet-the-parents thing I'd ever gone through had ended disastrously, with my parents certain their daughter had been brainwashed by a godless individual and my boyfriend kicking me to the curb because I had too much baggage.

My baggage was named Betty and Mick and came wearing polka dots and sweater vests on the way home from bridge club. Sometimes it was hard to believe that I came from them. The first time I dyed my hair bright pink, my mom burst into tears, like I told her I was sixteen and pregnant. And that was only temporary dye.

It was easier these days just to humor them, especially since they were still helping me out financially so I could spend more time working on my music. And it wasn't that I didn't love them . . . I did. I just didn't love the person they wanted me to be.

So, I made small sacrifices. I didn't introduce them to my boyfriends. I dyed my hair a relatively normal color before any trips home. I took out or covered my piercings and wore long-sleeved, high-neck shirts to cover my tattoos. I told them I worked the front desk at an accounting firm instead of a tattoo parlor, and never mentioned my other job working in a bar.

When I went home, I played at normal for a few days, and then got the hell outta Dodge before my parents could try to set me up with a crusty accountant.

"Yes, Mom. The library."

When I went home for Christmas, I'd just tell her it didn't work out with the library boy. Or that he was a serial killer. Use that as my excuse to never date nice guys.

"Well, that sounds lovely. We'd love to meet him."

Mace returned to me then with my purse and our coffees. He snuck a flask out of his pocket and added a little something special to his drink. I waved him off when he offered it to me. The caffeine was enough. Funny how he couldn't afford coffee, but he could afford alcohol.

"Sure, Mom." Mace snuck a hand into my coat and wrapped it around my waist. His hand was large and warm, and his touch through my thin tee made me shiver. "I think you would actually really like him." I finished the sentence on a breathy sigh as Mace's lips found the skin of my neck, and my eyes rolled back in bliss. I'd never met an accountant who could do *that*. "He's very, ah, talented."

"I guess we'll see for ourselves soon." Dad's reply was gruff.

Hah. If they thought there was any chance I was bringing a guy home for Christmas, they were delusional.

"Sure, Dad."

Mace's lips were making a pretty great case for skipping this morning's band practice, but it was our last time to practice all together before our gig next week.

"Great," Dad said. "We'll be at that coffee place in about five minutes."

My coffee hit the floor before I even got a chance to taste it.

"You WHAT? You're not at home in Oklahoma?"

Mace jumped back when the coffee splattered all over our feet. "Jesus, Max!" I didn't have time to worry about him. I had much bigger issues.

"Don't be mad, honey," Mom said. "We were so sad when you said you couldn't come home for Thanksgiving, then Michael and Bethany decided to visit her family for the holiday, too. So we decided to come visit you. I even special ordered a turkey! Oh, you should invite your new boyfriend. The one from the library."

SHIT. SHIT. ALL OF THE SHITS.

"Sorry, Mom. But I'm pretty sure my boyfriend is busy on Thanksgiving."

Mace said, "No, I'm not." And I don't know if it was all the years of being in a band and the loud music damaging his hearing, or too many lost brain cells, but the guy could just not master a freaking whisper!

"Oh, great! We'll be there in a few minutes, sweetie. Love you, boo boo bear."

If she called me boo boo bear in front of Mace, my brain would liquefy from mortification. "Wait, Mom—"

The line went dead.

I kind of wanted to follow its lead.

Think fast, Max. Parentals in T-minus two minutes. Time for damage control.

Mace had maneuvered us around the spilled coffee while I was talking, and he was moving to put his arms back around my waist. I pushed him back.

I took a good look at him—his black, shaggy hair, gorgeous dark eyes, the gauges that stretched his earlobes, and the mechanical skull tattooed on the side of his neck. I loved the way he wore his personality on his skin.

My parents would hate it.

My parents hated anything that couldn't be organized and labeled and penned safely into a cage. They weren't always that way. They used to listen and judge people on the things that mattered, but that time was long gone, and they'd be here any minute.

"You have to leave," I said.

"What?" He hooked his fingers into my belt loops and tugged me forward until our hips met. "We just got here."

A small part of me thought maybe Mace could handle my parents. He'd charmed me, and for most people that was akin to charming a python. He may not have been smart or put together or any of those things, but he was passionate about music and about life. And he was passionate about me. There was fire between us. Fire I didn't want extinguished because my parents were still living in the past, and couldn't get over how things had happened with Alex.

"I'm sorry, babe. My parents have made an impromptu visit, and they're going to be here any minute. So, I need you to leave or pretend like you don't know me or something."

I was going to apologize, say that I wasn't ashamed of him, that I just wasn't ready for that. I didn't get a chance before he held his hands up and backed away. "Fuck. No argument here. I'm out." He turned for the door. "Call me when you lose the folks."

Then he bailed. No questions asked. No valiant offer to brave meeting the parents. He walked out the door, lit up a cigarette, and took off. For a second, I thought about following him. Whether to flee or kick his ass, I wasn't sure.

But I couldn't.

Now, I just had to figure out what to tell my parents about my suddenly absent library-going-nice-guy-boyfriend. I'd just have to tell them he had to work or go to class or heal the sick or something. I scanned the room for an open table. They'd probably see right through the lie and know there was no nice guy, but there was no way around it.

Damn. The coffee shop was packed, and there weren't any open tables.

There was a four-top with only one guy sitting at it, and it looked like he was almost done. He had short, brown curls that had been tamed into something neat and clean. He was gorgeous, in that all-American model kind of way. He wore a sweater and a scarf and had a book sitting on his table. Newsflash! This was the kind of guy libraries should use in advertising if they wanted more people to read.

Normally I wouldn't have looked twice at him because guys like that don't go for girls like me. But he was looking back at me. Staring, actually. He had the same dark, penetrating eyes as Mace, but they were softer somehow. Kinder.

And it was like the universe was giving me a gift. All that was missing was a flashing neon sign above his head that said ANSWER TO ALL YOUR PROBLEMS.

ABOUT THE AUTHOR

CORA CARMACK is a twenty-something writer who likes to write about twenty-something characters. She's done a multitude of things in her life—retail, theatre, teaching, and writing. She loves theatre, travel, and anything that makes her laugh. She enjoys placing her characters in the most awkward situations possible, and then trying to help them get a boyfriend out of it. Awkward people need love, too.

Visit www.AuthorTracker.com for exclusive information on your favorite HarperCollins authors.